Locked In

Gabriel Lovemore

If you can feel it on the inside
You never have to wonder where the groove
went
The groove is you.

Deep Dive Corp

Acknowledgments

I'd like to express my gratitude to Betsy Chasse for guiding this book into the world. To Camille Deprez and Cathy Hacker, for reading early drafts and telling me the truth. To Louise Cottrell, for introducing me to Justin Faerman.

Justin Faerman, for the framework that sparked it all. His paper, Mapping the Evolution of Consciousness, synthesized decades of developmental psychology and consciousness research into something I could actually use—and more importantly, share. This book wouldn't exist without his work. Thank you for letting me play with it.

To Sri Aurobindo, Rudolf Steiner, Carl Jung, Jean Piaget, Abraham Maslow, Erik Erikson, Clare Graves, Jean Gebser, David Hawkins, Ken Wilber, and the countless others who mapped the territory before me. I stood on your shoulders for a moment. I hope I didn't scuff the view.

And to every species on this planet—animal, plant, mineral—carrying the burden of what humans have become. I'd promise to do better, but I know my species. That would be a lie. So, I'll just say: I see you. I'm sorry.

CONTENTS

FOREWORD BY JUSTIN FAERMAN

When I originally published the framework on which this book is based, one of my primary intentions was to create something that was both accurate to the actual territory of human psycho-spiritual development and not just an academic study, but also imminently practical and usable in one's day-to-day life.

When I first heard Gabriel's story of how he came to write this book, it was clear to me he had done just that: lived this framework day in and day out in his own life and in his professional work with others for many years, to such a degree that it had become an extension of his being and lived experience. Not only had he grasped the concepts and developmental framework masterfully, but he had run with it even further, made it his own, and brought it to life in meaningful ways, for many people—something which he has done beautifully once again with the artful weaving of the stories of the characters herein.

Told from the perspective of eight people trapped in a building during a climate crisis, Gabriel transports you into a raw, firsthand experience of what each level of consciousness is like in intimate detail through their unfolding responses to the day's events—not as abstract concepts, but as lived reality. Through their stories and experiences, a deeper truth is revealed: we do not see life as it is; we see it as we are, and thus, how we choose to see things can have wildly different outcomes played out across the trajectory of our lives.

While the levels of consciousness outlined in this book are first and foremost about one's own personal development and fulfillment, as go the individuals, so goes the collective. In the face of what can sometimes seem like the overwhelming or even insurmountable challenges that the world faces, there is perhaps no more radical act and contribution that you can make than your own inner shifts in perception and awareness—for these cannot help but echo out across your relationships, your community, and en masse, the world.

As such, my hope is that as you read this book, it nurtures your personal evolution, not only for yourself, but for us all. To that end, Gabriel has given us all a great gift: a roadmap disguised as a story. May it serve your journey well.

Author, "Mapping the Evolution of Consciousness: A Holistic Framework for Psychospiritual Development"
(https://www.justinfaerman.com)

Locked In

PREFACE

Twenty years as a spiritual teacher. Hundreds of clients.

Countless tools and frameworks.

And, if I'm being honest, most of them didn't stick. People politely smiled, took notes, and maybe felt inspired for a week. Some even told me how incredible the share was. Then they were off to the next "Thing". After years of doing all the "things", I started looking for something simpler, straightforward, even. I realized that sometimes the best answer is the one right in front of you, or in this case, all of you. The consciousness framework I share in this book is different. It is not sophisticated (in fact, it is quite simple), but it works. It's not trying to explain your life. It mirrors it, exposes it.

I found this model at the bottom of a rabbit hole that started with reading Ken Wilber. I followed the trail through Maslow, Graves, Steiner, and others. Developmental psychology. The research was mind-blowing.

The problem was delivery: who wants to read scientific papers in the age of Instagram memes? Anyway, academic papers don't change anyone. Not more than TED talks, if we're honest.

Information isn't enough for transformation.

Why does this matter? Because we're stuck. Not just personally, but most importantly collectively. The same patterns that keep Ray in his basement, blaming, and David in his penthouse, controlling, trap us in endless conflict: with each other, with ourselves, with the planet. Victims and dominators, locked in a dance for 10,000 years. And we keep trying to solve the mess with the same consciousness that created it. Understanding where we are isn't self-help. It's the first step out of a loop we've been running since the dawn of agriculture.

So, I was looking for something else. I wanted to do a quiz. A series of questions that direct our attention to the pain points we face in life. Finding out what our response says about our level of consciousness.

But building the questions was challenging, so I started visualizing different characters in my head, building their background, shadows, and gifts, trigger points, like one would do to create characters for a movie.

Picked eight characters. Set them in one building. Created one crisis. Showing eight completely different experiences of the same reality. After a while, I stood back, and I saw a book. One I had never thought of before.

The book came fast. Suspiciously fast. After years of starting projects that went nowhere, a memoir that stalled, a screenplay that died, three other books that fizzled, this one wrote itself in weeks. I didn't plan the structure. I didn't outline the plot. I did not describe my target audience. I just sat down, and it came out.

I don't say that to sound mystical. I say it because it startled me. Why did this work when previous projects had not?

Part of the answer was simple: those failures weren't failures. They were rehearsals. Every stalled project taught me what didn't work.

Every abandoned draft burned off something I needed to lose. I couldn't have written this book three years ago. I wasn't empty enough yet.

The other part came through the framework itself. My previous projects failed because I was writing from the wrong place, trying to prove something, and trying to be seen as the wise guy who got something others might want. Classic Level 2 and 3 bullshit, control, and self-image pretending to be creativity.

This book came from somewhere else. I don't fully understand where. Or I do, but it does not matter. Yet I trust this book more than anything I've written before.

The title arrived the same way. Someone asked if I had the story "locked in." The phrase hit me physically. Locked in, if you say it repeatedly, it sounds like a heartbeat, a rhythm line. My characters were locked in a building. But in music, "locked in" means the opposite of trapped. It means flow. The groove. When everything clicks.

Same words. Opposite meanings. Separated only by consciousness.

Yet I didn't fully get it until I wrote the scene between Marcus and Lucia. Two musicians who never played together. When they finally sat, their grief poured out, and years of silence broke open. I couldn't stop crying when I wrote their stories, and through the tears, I finally understood what "locked in" meant. Not an idea, more like a frequency, a groove. You either feel it, or you don't.

Locked In was the whole book in two words.

So, let me clarify this:

I've been every character in this story. I've been Ray, blaming the world for my pain. I've been David, grinding myself into the ground trying to control everything (and everyone). I've been Yara, bleeding out for people who didn't ask for my help. I have been Grace, sitting with the unfathomable grief of life, and Lucia, writing these lines without fully understanding what was going on. I've touched the other levels too, but I don't live there. Not consistently.

I'm still in it. Still failing. Still catching myself in patterns I thought I'd outgrown.

This isn't a book by someone who figured it out.

It's a book by someone who got tired of people pretending they do.

If that sounds like something you need, keep reading.

If you want inspiration without challenges, do us both a favor: put it back on the shelf

INTRODUCTION

I could tell you I've studied with the masters. It would be true. But who cares?

My credential is this one: the model works beyond the bubble.

Not just bougie cafes on the West Coast or yoga retreats in Costa Rica. It works in favelas, boardrooms, refugee camps, and prison cells. Our shared humanity doesn't care which side of the fence we were born on. A framework that holds across all borders isn't just interesting. It's proof.

You're about to meet eight people trapped in a building during a crisis. Same day. Same rain. Same power outage. Eight completely different experiences.

One drowns in blame. Another tries to control everything. A third takes radical responsibility. Another surrenders to what is. And one dissolves into pure presence.

By the end, you'll recognize yourself in all of them. Not just one.

All eight. And you'll see exactly where you live, and where you could go.

I could have written just a textbook. I didn't. Theory explains. Story transmits. This is both. When you read a definition of victimhood, you understand the concept. When you sit with Ray in the flooded basement, drowning in thirty years of invisibility, you feel it. You recognize it, in yourself, in people you know, in the parts of you that still believe life is happening to you.

These characters aren't metaphors. They're mirrors.

Everyone goes through these stages. Infants begin at Level 1, experiencing life as something that happens to them, entirely at the mercy of external forces. As they grow, they develop agency (Level 2), then self-awareness (Level 3), then trust (Level 4). Some people continue evolving, into surrender (Level 5), nondual awareness (Level 6), infinite possibility (Level 7), and unity consciousness (Level 8). Ray lives at Level 1. David at Level 2. And so on. You'll meet all eight.

Here's how this book unfolds:

Part I drops you into the story. Eight people, one building across six chapters. Each chapter captures a moment in time, all eight characters experiencing the same hour from eight different levels of consciousness. The same day. The same storm. Eight completely different realities.

Part II shows you a few examples of how I use the model in my life so you can see the map is real. You'll see where my voice comes from, and why I trust this framework.

Part III gives you the framework. The research. The theory behind what you just experienced through the characters. This is where you'll understand what you felt.

Part IV brings it home. What you do now. How to work with this. Where to begin.

Don't skip to the framework. Live the story first.

The theory lands differently after you've felt it.

No one occupies just one level. We move between them. Under stress, we regress. In flow, we expand. The work isn't to transcend the lower levels; it's to integrate them.

This framework isn't dogma. It's a map. A way to see where you are, where you've been, and where you could go. Yet reading the map isn't walking the terrain.

You can agree with everything in this book and stay exactly where you are.

Most people will. It's fine. This book isn't for most people.

PART I

CHAPTER I - 6:00 AM

6 am. The seventh day.

For the past six days, the heat did not break, nor did it ease. It was relentless. On day two, the AC failed. Day three, the backup generator died, and that was just before the riots started, six blocks away. People were shouting, and glass was breaking.

By day five, the National Guard had arrived. Young men in body armor, rifles across their chests, setting up barriers at the intersections.

The building had gone quieter than usual. Like holding its breath. Outside, the news cycled endlessly: the hurricane tearing up the coast in the south, politicians screaming at each other with the election six weeks out. Everyone was using the crisis to score points.

Inside, the building was falling apart, piece by piece.

Dark clouds gathered on the horizon. The air was thick, waiting. Something was coming. Holding its breath.

RAY - *Storage Room, First Floor*

And Ray Kowalski was the one trying to hold it together.

He woke to his phone buzzing on the metal desk. Three missed calls from the landlord.

He didn't need to listen to the voicemails. He already knew. Something was broken, someone was complaining, and it was his fault.

The cot creaked as he sat up. His back hurt, ever since he'd started sleeping here. Four months ago, after the rent on his studio went up, he couldn't make it work anymore. The building had this storage room behind his office, barely bigger than a closet. The landlord didn't know. Or didn't care. Probably both.

Forty-three years in this country. Forty-three years since he'd fled Poland during martial law, thinking America would be different. He'd been a teenager then, young enough to believe the propaganda about freedom and opportunity.

Warsaw, 1981. Tanks in the streets. Curfews. Solidarity crushed. He'd left everything, his mother, his sister, the apartment he'd grown up in, and gotten on a bus heading west.

And for what?

To end up here. Sleeping in a storage closet. Watching armed soldiers patrol American streets just like they had in Poland.

Ray splashed water on his face from the utility sink. The mirror showed what it always showed: a tired man who looked older than his age. Thinning hair. Bags under his eyes. The uniform shirt was already damp with sweat, even though he'd only been awake two minutes.

He pulled on his pants, clipped the radio to his belt, grabbed his clipboard. The work orders from yesterday were still there, seventeen of them. He hadn't finished even half.

The service elevator had been grinding for two days. Metal-on-metal sound that made people wince. He'd put up an "Out of Service" sign, but people used it anyway. What was he supposed to do, stand guard?

The city sent a notice about water restrictions. Twenty percent reduction or fines. How was he supposed to enforce that? Stand outside shower stalls with a timer? And the landlord, new owners, some investment group that bought the building two months ago, they were "reviewing operations."

Ray knew what that meant.

When he stepped into the basement hallway, the heat hit him like a wall. Worse down here. No windows, no air flow. Just concrete holding the temperature like an oven.

Marcus was at his desk, still as a statue, watching his monitors.

"Morning," Ray muttered.

Marcus nodded. Didn't say anything.

Ray climbed the stairs to the lobby. His knees ached. Everything ached.

The TV above the front desk was on, the news playing to an empty room. Same footage looping. The heat wave. The riots. The hurricane. Politicians shouting.

Ray stopped, watched for a moment.

They were all the same. East or west didn't matter. The people at the top stayed at the top. The people at the bottom got crushed.

He walked to the window. Outside, the sky was dark. Clouds, thick and low. The forecast said it will rain today, finally. But it also warned of flooding. Streets couldn't handle it after this much heat. The ground was too hard, the drains too clogged.

Of course. Six days of heat and now a flood.

The lights flickered.

Ray looked up. The chandelier in the lobby dimmed, buzzed, then came back.

Brownout. The grid barely holding on.

Everything falling apart at once.

And somehow, it would all be his fault.

DAVID - *4th floor Penthouse*

David woke fifteen minutes before his alarm. As usual.

The penthouse was dark, temperature-controlled, silent. Floor-to-ceiling windows overlooked the city, but the blackout shades were down. He didn't need to see outside. He already knew what was there: things were out of control.

He sat up, checked his phone. Forty-three emails since midnight. Three from the board. One from his ex-wife about next month's custody schedule. He deleted that one without reading.

Emotions were a luxury. His parents had taught him that. They'd crossed an ocean with nothing, worked jobs that broke their bodies, saved every dollar.

His mother still didn't speak English after forty years in this country. Didn't need to. She'd raised him in Mandarin, in silence, in discipline. His father's only advice: "Life is hard. You work harder."

David had. MBA at twenty-five. First company at twenty-eight. Sold it at thirty-five. Now he ran the investment arm, controlled millions, lived in a penthouse his parents would never understand.

But their ethos lived in his chest.

The gym was in the corner of the bedroom, with an exercise bike, weights, and a yoga mat. He changed into shorts and spent thirty minutes on the bike, watching the resistance numbers climb. His heart rate peaked at 168. Good. He needed the burn. Needed to feel his body obeying what he told it.

His jaw ached. He'd been grinding his teeth again. Woke up with headaches three times this week.

Shower. Protein shake. Charcoal suit, white shirt, no tie. By 6:30, he was in his office, screens awake, markets opening in New York, already opened overseas...

The news was on mute in the corner. Same footage looping: the whole country was a powder keg.

David didn't watch. He tracked futures. The energy sector down twelve percent. Green tech up nine. The UN climate report had not yet been released, but its imminent release already tanked fossil fuel stocks overnight. Predictable. He'd moved his portfolio three days ago.

His phone buzzed. A text from James, the board chair.

Emergency meeting. 1 pm today. Video call.

David's jaw tightened. Emergency meeting. That meant the quarterly numbers were worse than projected. That meant they were questioning his strategy. That meant they were questioning him.

He texted back: *I'll be there.*

The morning blurred. Calls with analysts, emails to department heads, spreadsheets that didn't add up the way they should. The company was solid; he'd built it, but the market was irrational.

You couldn't predict chaos. You could only position yourself to survive it.

YARA - *Apartment #11, First Floor*

Yara woke up to a text from a client: '*I can't do this anymore.*'

She sat up, heart already racing. Checked the name. Devon. Twenty-three, depression, history of attempts. They'd had a session two days ago, and he'd seemed stable. Better, even.

She texted back: *I'm here. What's happening?*

The dots appeared. Disappeared. Appeared again.

Nothing came through.

Yara called. Straight to voicemail.

She got out of bed and paced to the window. The heat was ever-present, even at dawn. Six days of it. She loved the heat; it reminded her of her childhood in Egypt, but here it was different. After three days, she'd stopped sleeping well.

Her body wouldn't settle, her mind wouldn't quiet. Every night she lay awake cataloging her failures, her patterns, the ways she kept choosing the wrong men, the ways she still flinched when her mother called. She kept choosing men who needed fixing. Told herself it was love when it was security, sort of, you can't be rejected by someone who needs you.

She was a therapist. She should have this figured out by now.

Her mother would have laughed at that. Figured out?

In their house in Alexandria, nothing was ever figured out. There was only the next guest, the next gathering, the next person who needed tea, conversation, and a place to feel welcome. Yara had grown up learning to read rooms, to sense what people needed before they asked. Her mother called it hospitality. Yara had turned it into a career.

But somewhere along the way, the giving had become compulsive. She didn't know how to stop.

She tried Devon again. Voicemail.

She texted: *Please call me. Or text. Just let me know you're okay.*

The dots appeared. Then vanished.

Yara stood at the window, phone pressed to her chest, willing it to buzz.

After an hour, she gave up trying to sleep and made coffee. The kitchen was a mess, dishes piled in the sink, the counter cluttered with half-opened mail, and a stack of books she kept meaning to read. She told clients their apartment reflected their inner states. But her own apartment looked like someone was barely living in it.

She sat at her desk and pulled out her journal. The morning pages ritual she'd kept for six years—three pages, whatever comes, no editing.

Devon. I can't reach him. I'm scared. What if...

She stopped. Put the pen down.

She picked up the pen again.

The heat is making everything worse. Everyone's on edge: the riots, the violence. My parents called last night, asking if I was safe. I said yes, but I don't feel safe. I don't know if anyone does.

Her phone buzzed. She grabbed it.

Not Devon. A news alert. The hurricane.

Yara set the phone down and closed her journal.

She'd been reading about climate grief. How to talk about it without making it worse. But she didn't know how to hold it herself. Every time she read the news, she felt the weight of it, this massive, unstoppable thing bearing down on everyone, and what was she supposed to do? Recycle? Vote? Tell her clients to breathe through it?

She showered. Even the cold water was lukewarm. The building's system couldn't keep up with the heat. She stood under the stream, eyes closed, trying to find her center.

But it felt like hers. Devon. The climate. Her mother's disappointment that she still wasn't married. Her father's silence. The way her last relationship had ended with him saying, *'You're never actually present, you're always in your head analyzing everything. You don't want a partner. You want a patient.'*

She understood why he would say that.

GRACE - *Apartment #21, Second Floor*

Grace woke before the sun. A lifelong habit. Trained to be ready early, part of her hospice life.

She lay still for a moment, listening. The building was quiet except somewhere, far below, the faint sound of people moving through the building.

The heat had been hard, but Grace had lived through worse. War. Displacement. A husband's slow death from cancer. Six days of California heat was nothing.

She sat up slowly, joints stiff but cooperative. The diagnosis had come back three weeks ago. The cancer—kidney, stage four—had returned. Six months, maybe less. The oncologist had used words like "aggressive" and "treatment options," but Grace had worked hospice for thirty years. She knew what those words really meant.

She wasn't afraid.

She made tea. Rooibos, honey, oat milk. Sat by the window with her hands wrapped around the warm cup, watching the sky, darker than usual for this time of the day. The city below, streetlights glowing orange through the heat haze.

She noticed the plants were struggling. She watered them carefully, touching each leaf, whispering encouragement. The Ficus had dropped half its leaves. The jade plant was shriveled. But the succulent—stubborn little thing—was holding on.

"You and me both," Grace said softly.

She called her daughter in Seattle.

"Mama, are you okay? I saw the news..."

"I'm fine, baby. The rain is coming today. The heat will break."

"You should leave. Come stay with us. Just for a few weeks until..."

"I'm not leaving."

Her daughter sighed. Grace could hear the worry in it, the frustration. Her children wanted to fix things, to protect her. They didn't understand yet that some things couldn't be fixed. Some things just had to be walked through.

"I love you," Grace said. "Tell the kids I'm thinking of them."

After she hung up, Grace sat in her chair, looking at the photos on the wall. Her late husband, smiling in their wedding photo. Her three children at various ages. The patients she'd sat with in their final days, some had sent her pictures afterward, their families wanting her to know how much it had mattered that she'd been there. No photos from before. From Congo. From the life before this one.

She sat with that for a moment. Then her mind went where it always went: the work. Decades in hospice, hundreds of patients. At first, she'd tried to offer comfort, the right words, something meaningful. Eventually, she realized there were no right words. She just held people's hands and said, "I'm right behind you."

Now she was the one just behind.

She touched the small lump under her ribs, the place where the cancer was growing. She could feel it now, a subtle pressure. No pain yet.

"Okay," she said quietly. "I see you."

LUCIA - *Apartment #22, Second Floor*

Lucia woke to the sound of rain. Just a few drops carry the promises of relief from the heat. The sharp notes of a music that had been waiting all week to play. She lay still. Didn't move.

The heat wave would break. She could feel it in the air, something releasing, something shifting. Her body knew before her mind did.

Her phone was silent, but she could see the glow on the nightstand. She'd seen the notifications before falling asleep. Rico at the club. Her mother. Several missed calls.

Tour starts in three weeks. Need your answer by tonight.

Mija, your father fell again.

She turned away from the phone. Not yet.

The rain kept falling. Lucia closed her eyes and let it wash through her. The question was already there: tour or stay, go or root, but she didn't have to answer it yet.

She could just listen. Just float. Just be here, in this bed, in this rain, without deciding anything.

That was the gift. And the trap.

She knew she avoided things. The tax forms piled on her desk. The leak in the bathroom she kept meaning to report. The conversation with her mother she'd been dodging for weeks.

She was good at feeling. Good at playing. Good at letting music move through her like water.

She was not good at choosing. At logistics. At the hard edges of life that didn't bend to intuition.

She'd learned the hard way to wait. Her head could decide in seconds. Her body took days. She'd wrecked things by moving too fast, trusting the wrong voice.

The tour was a hard edge. Her father's illness was a hard edge. Even Daniel, sweet, patient Daniel, was becoming an edge. *Where is this going?* He'd asked last week, gently, and she'd kissed him instead of answering.

A kiss was a good way out.

Daniel was new, three weeks in, still uncertain. Before him, two years of nothing. And before that, David from upstairs, a few nights that went nowhere.

The rain drummed on. Lucia pulled the blanket higher.

Not yet. She'd deal with it at nine. Or ten. Or whenever her body finally made her rise.

For now, she just listened to the music, the rhythm. Heartbeat. Raindrops.

ANJALI - *Apartment #31, Third Floor*

Anjali had not used an alarm for years.

She sat up in darkness, bare feet on the cool wood floor, and breathed. Three breaths. Slow, complete, aware.

The heat had been present all week; she didn't mind, didn't resist it. It was nothing if you'd been raised in Mumbai.

She walked to the small altar in the corner of her bedroom. Lit a candle. Incense, sandalwood, simple. Sat on her cushion facing east, spine straight, hands resting in her lap.

Forty minutes of sitting. No timer. Her body knew when it was complete.

During the sit, the mind wandered as it always did—thoughts about the heat, the news, the student who'd sent the email three days ago. *You sit there all peaceful while the world burns. What are you actually doing? This is spiritual bypassing.*

She tried to let them pass. It did not work. The words had landed. She couldn't pretend they hadn't.

She rose. Made tea. Chai, one piece of India she'd kept. Sat by the window with the cup between her palms, watching the sky lighten.

The student, Priya, twenty-eight, angry and brilliant, wasn't wrong. Not entirely.

Anjali had spent twenty years dissolving the small self, learning to rest in awareness, teaching others to do the same. She'd walked the path honestly. Therapy for the trauma. Shadow work for the bypassing.

But Priya's words still cut.

What are you actually doing?

She stood at the window, watching the first drops fall. The heat breaking. The city exhaling. She felt it in her body—release, relief—but beneath that, stillness.

The rain starting as she finished her tea, felt synchronistic. The world responding. Or her responding to the world. At this point, she couldn't tell the difference.

But was that enough?

Anjali showered. Cold water was always her preference. The body awakened, alert, alive.

She dressed in loose linen pants and a modern version of the traditional kurta. No jewelry except a small silver ring her mother had given her before she died. *Don't forget where you came from, beta.*

Anjali hadn't forgotten. Mumbai. The noise, the chaos, the poverty pressed against wealth. Her parents' tiny apartment, where she'd shared a room with two sisters. The pressure to marry, to have children, to be a proper Indian daughter.

She'd left at twenty-two. Came to the west for graduate school. Philosophy, then psychology, then meditation. The path had unfolded naturally, inevitably, like water finding its level.

Her parents had been devastated. Her father still didn't speak to her. Her mother had,

before she died, but always with sadness beneath the words.
You chose a lonely life, Anjali.

Maybe. Her mother called it loneliness. Anjali called it something else.

SAMIR - *Apartment #32, Third Floor*

Samir woke up early to the spins of his own mind.

The unstoppable hum of equations running like background music, wave functions collapsing into form, consciousness interfacing with the quantum field. Math was beautiful. Elegant. Terrifying.

And it pointed where he knew it would.

He sat up in bed, rescued the notebook from the sheets. Scribbled in the dark, handwriting barely legible. Seven years of work. Hundred pages of theory. And now, finally, a framework that held together.

Consciousness doesn't just observe reality. It participates in its creation.

He'd known this for years. Not from the equations. From experience.

His ex-wife had dragged him to a silent retreat. Ten days, no talking, no phone, no work. He'd resisted every minute, until day seven, when something cracked open. Twenty minutes? Maybe much longer. No "Samir observing reality". Just awareness. No boundary between inside and outside. No observer, no observed. Just... this.

When it ended, he wept. He had never felt home like this before.

He'd spent years trying to prove what he'd experienced. Quantum mechanics, biocentrism, morphogenetic field theory. Building a framework that could hold the truth he'd touched.

The math worked. The logic was sound. But proof?

That was the problem. You couldn't prove this on a blackboard. You couldn't publish a mystical experience in a peer-reviewed journal. Hard science demanded external measurement, replicable experiments, and peer review. It had no room for interior experience, even if that experience had been reported by mystics across every culture for thousands of years.

Samir shook his head. He was a physicist, not an anthropologist. He needed proof. Real proof.

He got out of bed. His apartment was a disaster, whiteboards covered in equations, books stacked in towers, coffee mugs forming their own civilization on every flat surface.

He made coffee the only way he'd like, like Nescafé whipped with condensed milk until frothy. It reminded him of home, Nigeria. He stood at the window, looking out at the dark city.

The heat wave had been brutal. He hadn't noticed the AC was dead until his ex-wife called, asking if he was still alive. He'd been too absorbed in the work.

Seven years. And he still couldn't bridge the gap.

He knew the truth. He just couldn't prove it.

Not the way physics demanded.

MARCUS - *Basement*

For six days, Marcus had been sitting with the fever exhaled by the concrete at night. Upstairs, people could not sleep. He watched the building's movement on the monitors. People pacing, moving, trying something to escape their bodies.

Marcus sat in his chair in the basement, an open door, a subtle draft, finding the only cool place left in the building. The AC had failed, but it never reached here, so Marcus didn't mind. He just sat.

The screens glowed. Tiny squares of light, each one a window, a different point of view on life. How long had he been working here? He had forgotten. Long enough to know everyone, their rhythms, their attitudes. He felt everything like a pulse, the complaints of Ray, echoing the grind of the elevator. Marcus had a sweet spot for Ray; he reminded him of what life could be like when you don't pay attention. David, the fast-paced human, always running, no stillness in him. Yara, the therapist, with a heart like a marshmallow. He'd met them all, helped them all at one moment or another.

The heat broke everything, but mostly everyone. The riots were placing everyone on edge; it was so close you could hear the crowd, and you could feel the stress crescendo in waves. The building's nervous system is on edge, its arteries about to burst, awaiting the stroke or a nervous breakdown.

Then the Guards came. How could anyone feel safer with more guns around? This Marcus never understood. People stopped lingering, people would hurry, hide, avoid…

Marcus watched it all. The fear moving through the building like a current.

He felt it. It would pass.

CHAPTER II - 9:00 AM

9 am. The rain came without warning.

After six days of heat, the sky finally cracked
open. At first, it was a relief.
Quickly, the relief turned to downpour.

The UN climate report hit the headlines,
confirming the worst projections. We had
long passed the point of no return. The news
split screens, hurricane footage on one side,
graphs and predictions on the other.

In the building, people watched from their
windows.
Some hoped the rain would break the
tension.
Others feared it would bring more chaos.

The sky showed no sign of stopping.
And what was hidden started to show.

RAY - *Storage Room*

Ray's radio crackled. "Ray, you there?"

First floor. The therapist. Yara.

He keyed the mic. "Yeah."

"My sink is backing up. There's water all over the floor."

"I'll be right there."

Yara's door was open. She was standing in her kitchen, barefoot, holding a towel. Water pooled around the base of the sink, dripping onto the tiles.

"I don't know what happened," she said. "I was just washing a cup and..."

"It's the building," Ray said. He knelt and opened the cabinet under the sink. The pipe was leaking where it connected to the wall. Old seal, dried out from the heat. He didn't have a replacement. He'd ordered parts three weeks ago, and they still hadn't come.

He grabbed a roll of plumber's tape from his tool bag, wrapped the joint, tightened it as much as he could. The leak slowed but didn't stop.

"Try not to use the sink until I can get a part."

Yara frowned. "How long?"

"I don't know."

She didn't say anything, just looked at him, waiting for more. As if he were supposed to have an answer.

He stood. "I'll let you know."

Back in the hallway, his phone buzzed. Text from the penthouse. David Chen.

Ceiling leak. Need you immediately.

Ray stared at the screen. The penthouse. Of course. The richest guy in the building and his ceiling was leaking.

He took the stairs. Four flights. His legs burned by the second floor.

The penthouse door was already open. Expensive furniture. Floor-to-ceiling windows. A brown water stain spreading across the white ceiling like a bruise.

David was at his desk, laptop open, barely looked up. "It's getting worse."

Ray set down his toolbox. Pulled a bucket from the utility closet. Put it under the drip.

"I checked earlier, roof drains are clogged," Ray said. "I'll clear them when the rain stops."

"When it stops?" David looked up now. "I have a meeting in an hour. I need this fixed."

"Can't go on the roof in a storm, that is a safety rule."

"That's unacceptable."

Ray felt heat in his chest. Thirty years of this. People who thought money bought miracles.

"I'll do what I can," he said flatly.

"I'm calling the landlord."

"You do that."

Ray left. Climbed back down the stairs, legs shaking now.

Of course, David would call the landlord. Of course, he'd complain. They had problems; they made calls. People got fired.

People like Ray.

His phone buzzed again. The musician on the second floor, toilet wasn't flushing.

Ray closed his eyes. Took a breath.

He was on the roof earlier, checking the drainage vents, when he felt the first drops on his neck, cool and startling after so many days of heat.

He looked up. The sky was black, swirling. The wind was picking up.

The rain was intensifying by the minute.

Ray climbed down the ladder, soaked before he even reached the stairwell.

The roof drains were clogged just like he knew they'd be; he could see water pooling in the low spots. It will overflow soon. Leak into the top floors.

More work orders. More complaints. More calls to the landlord about the useless building manager who couldn't keep a roof from leaking.

Back in the lobby, Ray stood dripping on the tiles, watching the rain through the window.

The streets would be flooded soon. Water was already over the curbs, filling the gutters.

And three blocks down, past the barriers, he could see them: National Guard trucks. Soldiers in formation. Setting up positions as if they were expecting a war.

Ray's chest tightened.

He'd seen soldiers in the streets before. The government said it was for everyone's safety. For order. For protection.

Right before they started arresting people.

His radio crackled. Another complaint. Another problem he couldn't fix.

The world was falling apart.

And somehow, he was supposed to hold it together with duct tape, sheer will, and the occasional Polish curse.

It wasn't enough.

It was never enough.

DAVID - *Penthouse*

David stood at the window, shades up now, watching the storm roll in. The sky was black, the clouds moving fast. The first drops cracked against the glass.

He liked storms. He liked their power.

His phone buzzed. His ex-wife.

Kids want to know if you're coming to Maya's recital next week.

He stared at the text. The piano recital. He'd forgotten.

I'll try.

He knew he wouldn't. There was always something. A meeting, a call, a crisis. And honestly, sitting in a middle school auditorium watching twelve-year-olds butcher Mozart wasn't where he needed to be. His time was worth more than that.

He paid. Child support on time, every month, more than the court ordered. Private school tuition covered. College fund growing, fully on track. That was his role. Provide. Protect. That's what his father had done. Work hard, make money, take care of your family. The rest were details.

David walked back to his desk. Pulled up his presentation for the board meeting. The recovery strategy. The pivot plan. Three scenarios, contingencies built in. He ran through the numbers again. Revenue projections, cost cuts, timeline to profitability.

James would push back on the timeline. David rehearsed the response: *We can accelerate, but it increases risk. I don't recommend it.*

Firm. Confident. In control.

That's when he noticed the leak. A brown stain was spreading across the white ceiling above his desk.

He grabbed his phone, texted the building manager and left the door open.

Ray showed up minutes later, set a bucket under the drip. And left.

David's jaw tightened. His work was important. He didn't have time for details on someone else's to-do list. He grabbed the phone.

Unacceptable. He paid a premium for everything. Premium rent for the penthouse. Premium building fees. He deserved basic competence. He pulled up his contacts. Called building management.

"This is David Chen in the penthouse. Your building manager just refused to fix a leak in my ceiling. I'm paying top-tier rent for this unit, and I expect immediate service. The roof needs to be fixed. Now."

"Mr. Chen, we'll look into it…"

"Don't look into it. Handle it. I want confirmation within the hour that this is being addressed."

He hung up.

David turned back to his presentation. Tried to focus.

But his mind kept spinning. The board meeting. The leak. His ex-wife. His children. So much depended on him. The numbers that didn't add up. James questioning his strategy. The investors getting nervous.

He could manage this. He always managed it. You just had to think three steps ahead. Control the variables. Anticipate the objections.

Revenue down eighteen percent.

He'd spin it. Market volatility. External factors. The plan was sound.

Subscriptions bleeding.

Temporary. The pivot would fix it.

Talking about bringing in someone else.

They wouldn't. They needed him. He built this. He sold it. He knew every detail, every relationship, every…

Water dripped onto his desk.

Now his chest was tightening.

He couldn't control the rain. Couldn't control Ray. Couldn't control whether the board trusted him.

But he could control his presentation. His responses. His strategy.

He sat back down. Pulled up the slides.

Focused.

The meeting was in four hours.

He'd be ready.

YARA - *Apartment #11, first floor*

She had three clients scheduled for video calls. The first one canceled, couldn't handle the heat, wanted to reschedule. The second talked about her marriage falling apart.

Yara listened, reflected, asked questions.

But she also knew what she wasn't doing.

The client's husband was clearly manipulative. The patterns were textbook. Yara could see it, had seen it for months. But every time she got close to naming it, she softened. Reframed. Asked another open-ended question instead of saying what needed to be said:

You're afraid of losing him. But you're losing yourself.

She didn't say it. The session ended with the client feeling heard but no closer to the truth.

Between sessions, she went to wash her coffee cup. The sink gurgled, then backed up, murky water pooling around the drain.

She called Ray. *Ray, you there? My sink is backing up.*

He showed up ten minutes later, looking exhausted. He muttered something she couldn't hear, kneeling under the sink.

Yara hovered. "Can I help? Hold something?"

Ray glanced up. "I got it."

"I could…"

"I work better alone."

Yara stepped back. Felt the sting of it. Irrational, she knew. He was just doing his job. Her stomach tightened—same old reflex.

Ray wrapped some plumber's tape around the joint. "That's the best I can do right now. Try not to use the sink."

What kind of solution was that, but Ray was already gone.

The third client cried for forty minutes. Climate anxiety. Couldn't sleep. Couldn't imagine bringing kids into this world. Yara offered tools. Breathing exercises. Reframes.

But inside, she felt it too. The same fear. The same hopelessness.

When the session ended, Yara sat at her desk, staring at the wall.

She was supposed to have answers. That's what people paid her for. But she didn't have answers. She had questions. Doubts. A growing sense that all the therapy, all the inner work, none of it mattered if the world was burning.

And even if it did matter, was she actually helping anyone? Or just making them feel comfortable while they stayed stuck?

She glanced at her phone—still nothing from Devon.

The sky outside had darkened.

Then the rain started.

GRACE - *Apartment #21, Second Floor*

Grace turned on the news. The UN climate report had just dropped. The anchors spoke frantically, asking scientists and politicians what could be done. The same message since the 80's that no one seemed to listen.

Grace watched without judgment. This was how systems collapsed. Not all at once, but in waves. Heat, rain, floods. Pressure, release, chaos.

She'd seen it before. When the war came to Congo. When death would come to the hospice. There was always a pattern. Always a rhythm.

Then the footage shifted.

Congo. Eastern provinces. Children in mines, pickaxes in small hands, dust on their faces. Coltan. Cobalt. The minerals that powered the phones, laptops, and electric cars that were supposed to save the world.

The anchor's voice: "The green transition comes at a cost. And that cost is paid by the world's poorest."

Grace set down her tea.

The faces. The same faces. Forty-five years and nothing had changed. Different war, different name, same suffering.

She thought of Marie. Eleven years old, running beside her through the smoke. Then gone.

I'll come back for you.

The promise she didn't keep.

Grace turned off the television. Sat in the silence.

After a while, she stood. Put on her shoes. Walked to the farmer's market three blocks away.

The first drops of rain were starting to fall. The market was half-empty; most vendors hadn't come. The few who had looked exhausted were selling wilted greens and bruised tomatoes.

Grace bought what she could. Thanked each vendor by name. Asked about their families. Listened.

This was what she could do. Small things. Present things. One person at a time.

On the walk back, she saw the National Guard setting up barriers at the intersection. More force trying to rule the chaos.

She walked past them.

But Marie's face stayed with her. And the question she hadn't asked herself in years:

Was staying here and finding peace enough? Or did I just stop trying?

LUCIA- *Apartment #22, Second Floor*

At nine, her body was finally ready to rise.

She pulled on a tank top and loose cotton pants. Walked barefoot to the window. The sky was dark, the rain falling in sheets.

Lucia opened the window. Cool air rushed in, carrying the smell of wet pavement and the sharp tone of ozone. She closed her eyes, let the rain touch her face.

Thank you, she thought. There was no one to thank, but she felt grateful for the rain.

She made coffee. Sat on the floor with her back against the couch.

The apartment was a mess. Unopened mail scattered across the floor, her saxophone case open by the window, clothes draped over chairs, candles burned down to nothing on the bookshelf. Daniel had laughed when he first saw it. "Creativity is explosive," he said with a smile. It may not have sounded like it, but in his words, it was a compliment.

She liked that about him. He didn't try to fix everything.

Her phone buzzed. Her mother. Again.

She answered.

"Mija, are you okay? I saw the news about the storm coming…"

"I'm fine, Mamá. Just rain."

"They said the streets will flood."

"I'm safe. I'm not going anywhere."

Her mother sighed. "You could come here. Stay with us for a while."

"I'm okay."

"You know what I mean."

Lucia did know. Her mother had never understood why she'd left, why she'd chosen music over stability, why she'd turned down the teaching job her tía had lined up. *You could have a real career, mija. Benefits. Retirement.*

But this was her real career. Playing at clubs that smelled like smoke and whiskey. Teaching private lessons to kids who couldn't afford conservatory. Waking up whenever her body said so and writing melodies no one might ever hear.

It did not offer much stability. It was movement instead; it was alive.

"Your father wants to talk to you," her mother said.

A rustling. Then her father's voice, slower than it used to be.

"Lucia. Your mother told me about the tour."

Her chest tightened. "Papá..."

"You should go."

"But..."

"We're fine. Your mother worries too much. You worked hard for this. Go play your music."

She could hear the tremor in his voice. Parkinson's stealing his steadiness, word by word. And underneath, the thing he wasn't saying: *I don't know how many more chances I'll have to tell you this.*

"I'll think about it," she said quietly.

"Don't think too much." He laughed, but it got caught in his throat. "You always think too much. Just play."

After she hung up, Lucia sat with her saxophone. Didn't play. Just held it.

The horn was cool in her hands. Familiar. The one thing that never asked her to decide, to explain, to justify. She could just put her lips to the mouthpiece and disappear.

But the question wouldn't disappear with her.

The tour. Three months across the country, then Europe. Playing with some of the best jazz bands in the world. Everything she'd worked for. Her dream. Freedom. What her parents had crossed a desert for.

Yet so far, she was only inclined to say no.

For what? A father who told her to go? A mother who'd never understand? A relationship three weeks old?

What's wrong with me?

She set the saxophone down. Looked at the rain.

She didn't watch much news. It made her feel heavy. Not because she didn't care, but because she cared too much. Because she couldn't hold it all and still make music. The music required space. Emptiness. Room for something to move through.

If she filled herself with the world's pain, there was no space left for the sound.

So she didn't fill herself. She floated. She avoided. She stayed empty.

And empty felt like freedom.

Other times, it felt like hiding.

ANJALI - *Apartment #31, Third Floor*

Anjali made breakfast. Upma, semolina with mustard seeds, curry leaves, and veggies. Ate slowly, tasting each bite, aware of the body receiving nourishment.

Her phone buzzed. The group text for her evening meditation class.

Is class still happening tonight? Power's out in my building.

Mine too.

Roads are flooding.

Anjali typed: *We'll meet if we can. If not, sit where you are. The practice doesn't need a room.*

She set the phone down.

The class had been meeting for three years. Seven regulars, a few drop-ins. Priya had been one of them until last week. The email had come the day after class. Long, raw, accusatory.

You teach us to sit with what is, but what IS is collapse. Climate catastrophe. Fascism rising. People dying. And you just sit there talking about awareness like that's going to save anyone. It won't. It's bullshit.

Anjali had read it three times. Sat with it. Felt the sting. The defensiveness rising. The urge to explain, to justify.

Then she'd let it pass.

But the question remained.

What are you actually doing?

She knew this fire. She'd been Priya once.

Twenty-three years old, walking the slums of Mumbai with food packets and righteous certainty. Villains to blame, victims to save, herself as the hero who would make it right. She'd worked until she collapsed. Fought until she burned.

Her teacher had a name for it. Helping was fine. Fixing wasn't. Fixing assumed brokenness, and that assumption was the wound itself. As long as you saw the world that way, you perpetuated the very suffering you were trying to end.

So she'd stopped. Not stopped caring. Stopped acting from that place. Learned to be present without wanting to change anything. To serve from stillness. To let action arise rather than force it.

It had taken years.
She'd thought she was free of it.

But Priya's words had cut deep. Why?

Anjali sat with the question. What was she not seeing? What hadn't she healed?

She noticed a thought arise: Priya will understand someday. And beneath it, something less clean. A whisper of superiority. Of being further along. Of having already walked the path, Priya was stumbling through.

She sat with that too.

And then another thought, quieter: What if you stopped being Priya because it was too painful?

What if this is just your wound and you pretend it's evolution?

She didn't push it away. She let it land.

The rain was also landing harder now.

SAMIR - *Apartment #32, Third Floor*

Samir sat at his desk, laptop open, staring at the title page.

Consciousness as Creative Interface: A Unified Framework for Quantum Observation and Biocentric Reality Formation

Two hundred and forty-seven pages, to be exact. Endless nights of work. The cornerstones of science at the edge of human knowledge. All of it pointing in the same direction.

Reality is participatory. Consciousness is the variable. We're not just observing the world, we're co-creating it.

Could he prove it?

It is one thing to point the finger at the moon. It is another to actually see the moon. He only had fingers and no moon.

Which meant…

Samir rubbed his eyes.

Which meant if he published, physicists would tear it apart in any peer review. "Speculative." "Pseudo-science." He could already hear them.

And if not dismissed, it could be weaponized. Used to blame. Used to justify the unjustifiable, like poverty, injustice, and inequality.

Or worse, they'd just ignore it. Another fringe paper gathering dust.

The rain started.

Samir stood at the window, watching the first drops fall. He could see the pattern in it. The chaos that wasn't chaos. Raindrops falling in clusters, influenced by air pressure, temperature gradients, quantum fluctuations at the boundary layer.

Everything connected. Everything entangled.

His gift and his curse. He saw patterns everywhere. Couldn't stop seeing them. Even when no one else could.

He thought about his daughter. Sixteen, brilliant, furious at the world. Last time they'd talked, she'd asked why he spent so much time on abstract theory when people were dying.

He didn't have a good answer.

He picked up his phone. Called Dr. Nakamura, his mentor, retired now in Hong Kong.

"Samir. It's the middle of the night here."

"I know. I'm sorry. But I am at a dead end."

Silence. Then: "The consciousness paper?"

"Yes."

"And?"

"It all points in the same direction. Consciousness participates in reality formation. Not metaphorically. Structurally."

"But?"

Samir paused. "But I can't prove it. Not the way physics demands."

Another silence. Longer.

"Have you considered," Nakamura said slowly, "that maybe physics isn't the right tool?"

"What do you mean?"

"You're trying to prove an interior experience with exterior measurement. That's like trying to weigh love on a scale."

He paused. "Maybe proof isn't the point, Samir. Maybe pointing is enough."

"Pointing doesn't get published in peer-reviewed journals."

"No. It doesn't." Nakamura's voice softened. "But it might be the only thing needed."

After he hung up, Samir stood at the window, watching the rain.

Maybe physics isn't the right tool.

At least he knew that part was true.

MARCUS - *Basement*

Marcus watched the world through the small basement window. Drops hitting pavement, like fingers tapping the rhythm of the music in his head.

Outside, the world was madness. The heat had done its work. Nothing out there he did not know. He'd walked down that road before.

Fifty years ago, a young man with fire in his chest stood on streets like these kids today. Shouted similar words. Felt the same rage. His father's church was ash. King was dead. And his father, his own father, still talked about love.

They'd fought. The last real conversation they ever had.

Love doesn't stop bullets, Dad.

No. But hate doesn't stop anything at all.

Marcus had walked out. Chose his path. The Black Panthers, the resistance. Angela Davis, also from Alabama. The fight. He thought he was going to change the world.

The world was about to change him.

The cell was eight by ten. Concrete walls. Iron bars. A small window, too high to see through. He'd drawn piano keys on a board, under his mattress. Sat there for hours, fingers moving, playing music no one could hear. Sometimes he wondered what would have happened if he'd kept the music and left the gun. Like his father. Like King.

His mother had shown him when she drew his first cardboard keys. *The music doesn't need a piano, baby. It just needs you.*

He was playing those silent keys when the guard told him his father was gone.

They didn't let him out for the funeral. He played all night. The silence his song. And somewhere in that darkness, he finally heard what his father had been saying all along.

Love wasn't weakness. It was the only thing that didn't break.

Anger burned everything. Including the one holding the match.

Marcus looked at the monitors. Ray was in the hallway, hunched, muttering, carrying his bitterness like a bag of stones.

The riots outside weren't new. Just the same pain repurposed. Life's cycles.

He couldn't help them if he wanted to. You can't pull someone out of this fire. His father couldn't pull him out. You had to walk through. Burn. And choose what to do with the ashes.

But you could sit with someone. Leave a door open.

The rain was falling harder now. His basement home reminded him of his cell. The same small window to the world. The same isolation. He was the one to watch guard now. In a different way.

The building creaked like an old boat. A pipe shuddered. The old bones holding steady, riding out the storm, keeping everyone safe inside.

Marcus felt it all. The fear upstairs. The anger outside. The grief he'd carried for years, now quiet, now composted into something useful.

His father's voice, still there, underneath everything:

Love, son. Just love.

He'd finally learned to listen.

CHAPTER III - 11:00 AM

By 11 a.m., the downpour had turned into a storm.

Soon, the water reached the curbs. Storm drains overflowed. The intersections became shallow lakes. The news showed footage from downtown, cars abandoned, people wading through streets, the mayor urging calm.

In the building, like in an old body, the pipes groaned. The basement started seeping.
The walls felt closer than before.
And the cracks widened.

RAY - *Lobby*

Ray's phone rang. Management.

He answered. "Yeah?"

"Ray, this is Patricia from building management." Cold voice. Corporate.

Never heard of Patricia before, he thought.

"We received a complaint from Mr. Chen in the penthouse about a ceiling leak that hasn't been addressed."

Ray's stomach dropped. "I told him I'd fix it when..."

"He says you refused to go on the roof."

"It's pouring rain. I can't..."

"Mr. Chen is an important resident. The leak is damaging his office. You need to address this immediately."

Ray looked out the lobby window. The rain was torrential. The streets were rivers.

"You want me to go on the roof? In this?"

"We need the issue resolved. That's your job."

The line went dead.

Ray stood there, phone pressed to his ear, staring at nothing.

Thirty years of doing what he was told. Fixing what they told him to fix. Going where they told him to go.

Didn't matter that it was dangerous. Didn't matter that it made no sense.

He was a tool. A thing they used. Invisible until something broke.

David made one phone call. One complaint from the penthouse. And management called Ray. Told him to risk his neck on a wet roof in a storm.

People with money had power. People like Ray had orders.

By noon, the streets were flooding. The National Guard reinforced their positions, setting up more barriers.

He should go up there. Do what they said. Like he always did.

But his hands were shaking. He was fuming.

Not from fear of the roof.

But from thirty years of being treated like he didn't matter.

He walked to the basement instead. Marcus was still at his desk, watching his monitors.

"Management wants me on the roof," Ray said. "In this."

Marcus looked at him. Didn't answer.

The water was seeping in through the foundation, darkening the concrete in the corners.

Ray sat on the bottom step.

One phone call from the penthouse and he was disposable.

Everything was flooding. Everything was breaking.

And he was still just the guy they called to fix it.

DAVID - *Penthouse*

The rain intensified. Within minutes, it was a deluge. David watched the streets below turn into rivers, cars crawling through water, people running with their umbrellas bent by the storm.

His phone rang. James again.

"Meeting moved up. We need to talk before the rest of the board joins."

David's stomach sank. "What's going on?"

"The investors are on my back. We need a plan, David. A real one."

"I have a plan."

"Then you'd better be ready to sell it. Because right now, they're talking about bringing in someone else."

The line went dead.

David stood at the window, phone in his hand, staring at the rain.

Someone else.

They were questioning him. After everything he'd built. After everything he'd sacrificed, his marriage, his kids, his health, they were talking about replacing him.

His chest tightened. He knew this feeling. Had felt it before, watching his father come home after being laid off from the factory. The shame. The fear. His mother crying in the kitchen, whispering about how they'd survive.

His father had worked seventy-hour weeks. Done everything right. And they'd replaced him anyway.

That night, his father had told him, "Never let them have power over you. Control everything, or you control nothing."

He turned back to his desk. Pulled up the presentation he'd been working on for weeks. His strategy was good. The logic was sound. They just had to trust him.

But they didn't trust him. That's why he had to fight for every decision, every move. That's why he couldn't relax, couldn't delegate, couldn't let anyone else touch the wheel.

Because the moment he did, they'd take it from him.

David sat down. Opened the slides. Started rehearsing his responses.

His hands were shaking. He hid them under his thighs.

One hour until the meeting.

He could do this. He'd done it before.

The rain pounded harder. The ceiling dripped steadily into the bucket.

Everything was spinning. All of it out of control.

David closed his eyes. Breathed.

He could manage this.

He just had to hold on.

One more hour.

YARA - *Apartment #11, first floor*

Yara stood at her window, watching the streets flood. People running for cover.

Inside, everything felt frozen.

Ray's words kept circling. *I work better alone.*

She knew it wasn't personal. He was exhausted, overwhelmed, doing his job. But the sting wouldn't fade. She'd wanted to help. He didn't want her help.

Her phone buzzed.

Devon.

I'm okay. Sorry. Just needed space.

Yara exhaled. Tears came, sudden and sharp.

Relief, yes. He was alive. He was okay.

But underneath the relief, something else.

He didn't need her; maybe he was also better alone…

She'd spent all morning with her phone clutched to her chest, imagining the worst, preparing to save him. And he'd just… needed space. Not her. Space.

She thought about her client. The one with the manipulative husband. Yara had stayed with her. But she hadn't helped. The woman had left no closer to the truth than when she'd arrived.

And the third client, crying about the climate, the future, the world falling apart. Yara had offered tools. Breathing exercises. Reframes. But she'd felt it too. The same terror. The same hopelessness. She had nothing to give that she wasn't also drowning in.

No one needed her. Maybe they never had.

Yara sat on the couch. Pulled her knees to her chest.

She desperately wanted to help. To contribute.

And now...

The building was flooding. The world was drowning. People were suffering everywhere. And she couldn't do anything. Couldn't help Ray. Couldn't save Devon. Couldn't even tell her client the truth.

The rain pounded against the windows.

Yara sat on the floor, tears streaming, useless.

GRACE - *Apartment #21, Second Floor*

Grace stood by the window, watching the streets fill up and the sky darken. Mechanically, she started washing the vegetables. She had done it countless times, but her mind was somewhere else.

Marie's face wouldn't leave.

Forty-five years. Grace had built a life around that absence. She'd wanted to be a doctor. Had dreamed of joining Médecins Sans Frontières, returning to Congo, healing her own people. Finding Marie.

But being a refugee did not help. No one believed she could pull this. Nursing was easier, faster. Then marriage came. Children. Bills. Her husband's illness. And somewhere along the way, the dream got folded up and put away.

She became a hospice nurse instead. Held the dying instead. Told herself that service here or service there was the same, that small things mattered.

And they did. She believed that.

But the children in the mines. The same dust, the same eyes. The same suffering. The same country bleeding for the world's comfort. Forty-five years and she'd done nothing for them.

I was going to go back. I was going to find her.

The rain hit the window harder now.

Grace had made peace with dying. She'd told herself that too. Six months, maybe less. She wasn't afraid.

But sitting here, she saw something she hadn't let herself see before.

Part of her was ready to die because it meant she could stop carrying the promise.

I'll find you, Marie. Finally. On the other side.

Was that acceptance? Was that surrender?

Was she at peace with her life? Or just tired of the weight of what she hadn't done?

The rain kept falling. The room grew darker.

Grace sat with the question. Knowing no answer would come.

LUCIA - *Apartment #22, Second Floor*

Lucia looked at the drifting cars, abandoned boats on a wild river.

She sat on the couch, saxophone across her lap. She hadn't played since this morning. The question was too loud.

Go.

Her head made the case. The tour was everything. Three months with the best in the world, and if it went well, she'd join them full-time. It wasn't a tour. It was an invitation to a different life. New cities every week. Recording sessions in studios she'd only seen in documentaries. A career with no ceiling.

And no roots.

Her parents had crossed a desert for this. Her tía had begged her to take the teaching job, stable, safe, and Lucia had said no. For THIS. For the chance to play on real stages, for real audiences, for something bigger than neighborhood clubs and private lessons.

And now it was here. And she was hesitating.

What's wrong with you?

She ran through the logic. Her father was sick, yes. But he told her to go. Her mother was exhausted, yes. But she'd never forgive herself if Lucia stayed out of guilt. Daniel was new, uncertain, maybe nothing.

Every reason to stay sounded like an excuse.

Go. This is what you wanted. Take it.

But her body wouldn't move.

She'd tried to draft the text to Rico. *Yes. I'm in. Count me in.* Her fingers wouldn't type it. Something in her chest locked up every time she got close.

She knew this feeling. It was the same feeling she got when a melody was wrong, when her head said *this works*, but her body said *no, not this, keep looking.*

She trusted that feeling when she played. She let it guide her through improvisation, through composition, through every musical choice she'd ever made.

But this wasn't music. This was life. And life had consequences.

What if I'm just scared?

What if staying wasn't alignment? What if it was fear? She'd done that before, told herself she was "following her gut" when really she was just avoiding something hard. The audition she didn't attend because it "didn't feel right." The conversations she sidestepped, the decisions she delayed, the edges she softened until they disappeared.

She was good at disappearing.

Maybe I don't want the tour because I'm afraid I'll fail. Afraid I'm not good enough. Afraid of being seen.

Her head nodded. That made sense. That was the safe story: that she was not worthy enough, that her hesitation was weakness, that she needed to push through and do the hard thing.

But her body still wouldn't move.

She put her hand on her chest. Breathed.

What's true?

The head screamed: *Go. Prove yourself. Honor their sacrifice. Be somebody.*

The body whispered: *Stay. This is home. You're already somebody.*

She didn't know which one to trust.

Outside, the rain fell harder. Inside, Lucia sat with the oldest battle she knew, the head pulling her toward a different life, the body anchoring her to this one.

She didn't have an answer.

But she knew she couldn't think her way to one.

ANJALI - *Apartment #31, Third Floor*

The rain intensified. Anjali stood at the window, watching the streets. People were scared, running, trying to get home before the rain got worse.

The news on her phone showed the hurricane tearing through the coast. Entire neighborhoods underwater. Families evacuating. Bodies being pulled from the water.

Anjali felt it. The grief. The helplessness. The rage that systems had failed so completely.

She didn't push it away. She let it move through. Tears came. She let them fall.

Then she sat on her cushion and breathed.

She thought of the Gita. Krishna's words to Arjuna on the battlefield: *Your right is to action alone, not to its fruits.*

She'd built her life on that teaching. Act without grasping. Serve without attachment. Let the results belong to something larger.

But Krishna also said: *Even I am never without action. For if I did not act, these worlds would fall into ruin.*

Even the divine acted. Even the source of stillness moved.
And the Tao: *When nothing is done, nothing remains undone.*

She'd quoted these lines a hundred times. They'd never felt this hollow.

She'd always understood this. Non-doing wasn't passivity. It was effortless action. Aligned action. Doing what arose naturally, without forcing, without grasping at outcomes.

But what was arising in her now?

Sitting? Teaching? Showing up for seven students on Tuesday nights?

The world was burning. Twenty million in Mumbai still in poverty. The climate collapsing. Fascism rising.

And she was here. On a cushion. In a quiet apartment. Watching the rain.

What is my action?

Priya wasn't wrong to want action. She was wrong about where it came from.

You didn't act because the world was broken. You acted because action arose. From stillness. From clarity. From seeing what was needed without the weight of having to save anything.

But had she been serving? Or had she been sitting in her apartment, calling stillness what was really withdrawal?

That was the knife's edge. And she couldn't pretend she knew which side she was on.

Even the wise are confused about action and inaction.

Quotes were easy. Answers were not.

SAMIR - *Apartment #32, Third Floor*

Samir paced. His apartment was small, eleven steps from the window to the back wall. He'd measured it once during a bout of insomnia.

The rain was getting heavier. He could hear it through the walls, the building's rhythm changing. Footsteps above. Voices below.

Nakamura's words kept circling.

Maybe physics isn't the right tool.

He stopped at the whiteboard. Seven years of equations. Elegant. Coherent. Pointing exactly where the mystics had always pointed.

And that was the problem, wasn't it?

They'd already pointed. For thousands of years. Across every culture, every continent, every century. Hindus called it samadhi. Buddhists called it shunyata. Sufis called it fana. Different words. Same experience. The dissolution of the boundary between knower and known.

Countless people. Thousands of years. No communication between traditions.

And they all reported the same thing.

If that wasn't verification, what was?

But science wouldn't accept it. It refused to accept that the laboratory could be internal.

Show me external proof.

The proof is internal. Look for yourself.

Samir stared at the whiteboard.

Trying to translate interior experience into exterior proof. Trying to make physics accept what physics couldn't contain.

Why?

The question surfaced like something rising from deep water.

Why did he need to prove what had been known for millennia? To convince whom? Skeptics who wouldn't look? Academics who couldn't see? His daughter, who thought he was wasting his life?

Or himself?

He thought about day seven. The retreat. Twenty minutes of no boundary. No observer, no observed. Just pure awareness.

His mind leapt to his daughter's voice: *"You waste time on theory while people die."*

The streets below were flooding. The world breaking. And here he was, trying to prove what couldn't be proven. Only lived.

The mind had infinite questions he didn't have an answer for.

MARCUS - *Basement*

The building was groaning and stirring. Marcus felt it in his chest. The way you feel weather in your bones before the sky changes.

He'd been all of it. Every floor of this building lived somewhere in his body.

The drowning first. Years when nothing he did mattered. When the world was rigged, and he was just another body it would crush. He could still taste that bitterness. The weight of invisibility.

Then the fire. The fist. The gun in his hand and the certainty that force was the only language power understood. He thought he was going to change the world. The world changed him instead. Eight by ten. Concrete walls. Three years to learn what his father already knew.

After the cell, he thought he'd learned. Came out softer. Wanted to help everyone.

Carried their pain as if it were sacred. Thought that was service. It wasn't. Just another way to burn, slower, but the same fire. Righteous exhaustion instead of righteous rage.

Then the opening. The pattern underneath. Every fall, a lesson. Every loss a door. He'd found peace in that cell, playing silent keys, his father's voice finally reaching him.

The music taught him to surrender. To let things move through. Not giving up. Just getting out of the way.

Then came the stillness. The temptation to stay there. To watch from a safe distance. He'd done that for years. Called isolation peace.

But was it peace? Or just a cleaner hiding place?

He didn't have answers. Just the sitting. The silence. The willingness to not know.

His father's voice, quiet underneath it all:

This is what I was trying to tell you, son.

I know, Dad. I see it now.

CHAPTER IV - 1:00 PM

At 1 pm, the power went out. The lights died. The TV went silent. The hum of the building ended. The elevator froze. The emergency lights flickered on in the stairwells, dim yellow, barely enough to see.

Outside, the rain was torrential now, sheets of water hammering the building. The streets below were flooded, cars abandoned, water up to their doors. The National Guard kept trying to control the intersections.

Inside, the silence was louder than the storm. Everything stopped.

RAY - *Basement*

He stood in the dark, listening to nothing. The heartbeat of the building, the baseline noise Ray had lived with for thirty years, stopped.

His phone buzzed. The landlord.

Ray stared at the screen.

This was it. They were calling to fire him. In the middle of a flood, power out, building falling apart, and they were going to tell him he was done.

He let it ring.

Once. Twice. Three times.

Voicemail.

His phone buzzed again immediately. Same number.

Ray's hand hovered over the screen.

He knew what they were going to say. *Ray, we appreciate your years of service, but with everything going on... we're making some changes... nothing personal...*

Thirty years. And it would end with a phone call he was too afraid to answer.

The phone stopped ringing.

Voicemail notification.

Ray didn't listen to it.

What was the point? Whether they fired him now or tomorrow, the result was the same. He'd be out. Homeless. Sixty-six years old with nothing.

He walked to the basement in the dim light.

Marcus was sitting in the dark, flashlight on his desk.

"Power's out," Ray said.

Marcus nodded.

"You think it's coming back?"

Marcus looked at him. Didn't answer.

Ray sat on the bottom step, head in his hands.

The sump pump was dead without power. The basement would flood. Then the first floor. Then…

He couldn't do this anymore.

He couldn't fix it. He couldn't stop it. He couldn't save the building or himself or anything.

Thirty years. And it all came down to this. Sitting in a basement, watching water creep across the floor, too afraid to answer the phone that would tell him he was done.

His phone buzzed again. Text this time.

Ray, meeting postponed. Roads flooded. We'll reschedule.

Ray stared at the screen.

Not fired. Not yet.

Just... postponed.

He should have felt relief, instead he felt nothing.

Marcus stood. Picked up his flashlight. Walked to the stairs.

"Where are you going?" Ray asked.

"Surely someone needs help."

Ray watched him climb, slow and steady, disappearing into the darkness above.

He sat alone in the dark basement, listening to the rain hammer the building, feeling the water rise.

Thirty years of fixing things.

And when it mattered most, he couldn't even answer the phone.

DAVID - *Penthouse*

David stood in the sudden silence, staring at the black screen of his desktop.

No.

He tried the power backup. Nothing. The whole building was down.

He grabbed his phone. Battery at forty-three percent. No WiFi. He switched to cellular, but the signal was weak, one bar, flickering.

The meeting was imminent. He needed WiFi. He needed the presentation. He needed…

He called his assistant. Voicemail.

He called James. It rang four times, then cut off.

He tried the elevator. Pressed the button. Nothing.

He was trapped.

The penthouse had stairs, an emergency exit only, locked from his side, but he'd never used them. He didn't even know if they worked.

David stood in the middle of his dark apartment, breathing hard.

This wasn't happening. This couldn't be happening. The meeting would determine whether he kept his position or lost everything, and he was stuck in a powerless apartment with no internet and a dying phone.

He pulled up the video conference app. Tried to connect. The call wouldn't load.

He tried again. Spinning wheel. No connection.

He threw the phone on the couch.

David paced. He could feel his heart rate climbing, the tightness in his chest. His hands were numb. He couldn't catch his breath.

This was supposed to be the safest place in the city. The highest floor. The best view. The most control.

And now he was locked in a glass box with no power, no connection, no way out.

He walked to the window. Pressed his hand against the glass. It was cool, wet on the other side, streaming with rain.

Below, people were moving. Figures in the streets. They were handling it. Moving. Doing something.

David stood frozen, looking down at them.

For the first time in years, he had no move to make.

No call to take. No deal to close. No strategy to execute.

Just the rain. The dark. The silence.

He hated it.

All the control. All the years of managing every variable, anticipating every threat, never letting his guard down. And none of it mattered. The power didn't care about his preparation. The rain didn't care about his strategy. The board wouldn't wait.

He sank onto the couch. Put his head in his hands.

This was what his father felt. This exact helplessness. The day they laid him off. The shame in his eyes when he came home.

David had spent his whole life making sure he'd never feel this.

And here it was.

He didn't know how long he sat there. Time had stopped meaning anything.

Then he heard it.

Faint. Rising through the floor. A saxophone.

Lucia.

He hadn't thought about her in months. Hadn't let himself. But now, in the dark, with nothing left to manage, her music found him.

He did not know what he was doing. It made no sense. She was a closed chapter. A mistake. A wound he'd never let himself examine.

But his body was moving already.

YARA - *Apartment #11, first floor*

Yara was still sitting when the power went out.

She listened to the rain. Reminding her of her own tears.

She was at the edge of something she knew well. That heaviness that swallowed days, sometimes weeks. She did not want to go there.

Okay. Breathe. You know how to do this.

She closed her eyes. Tried to find her center. The visualization she taught clients, roots growing down, breath flowing up. Grounded. Present. Calm.

It didn't work.

Her mind kept spinning. Devon. Ray. Her client's trapped marriage. The flooding streets. The world falling apart.

You're spiraling. Name it. Witness it.

She couldn't witness it. She was inside it.

She grabbed her journal. Tried to write.

I feel overwhelmed. I feel useless. I feel...

The pen stopped.

What's wrong with me?

She taught people how to do this. How to regulate. How to process. How to sit with their own pain without drowning.

And here she was. Drowning.

If I create my reality, then why can't I change this?

The thought twisted in her chest.

Still, she was sitting alone in a dark apartment, crying over a client who didn't need her, a building manager who didn't want her help, a world she couldn't save.

Maybe I'm just not good enough. I pretend to help others, but I can't even help myself.

She needed to move. Needed to be somewhere else. Anywhere else.

The thought of Anjali surfaced like a lifeline. The meditation teacher on the third floor. They'd spoken a few times; there was something about her presence, calm, grounded, still.

Yara grabbed her phone. Opened the door.

She climbed the stairs.

GRACE - *Apartment #21, Second Floor*

Grace didn't move. The refrigerator stopped. But the soup was ready. There was a strange silence except for the rain.

She sat in the dim light, hands in her lap.

The woman she could have been. She was thinking about her now. The one who went back. Who became a doctor, who searched until she found Marie, or found a grave, who served in the camps, held the children, did something.

That woman had existed once. Young Grace, full of fire, full of plans. Refugee papers in hand, English classes at night, dreaming of medical school.

What happened to her?

Life happened. That's what Grace had always told herself. Life, with its small emergencies, its daily needs, its gentle erosions. You make choices. You build what you can. You accept what you can't change.

But acceptance was supposed to bring peace. And right now, sitting in the dark, Grace didn't feel peace.

She felt the weight of fifty years of not going back.

I told myself I was at peace with dying. But maybe I was just relieved.

Relieved to finally stop carrying it. Relieved to let death do what she couldn't—end the waiting, close the loop, reunite her with Marie without having to earn it.

That does not feel like acceptance. That feels like giving up.

Outside, the rain kept falling. Inside, Grace sat with the hardest truth she'd ever faced:

She had built a good life. A meaningful life. She had helped people, loved people, raised children, and held the dying with grace.

And she had also abandoned her sister. Her people. Her calling. Herself.

Both things were true.

She was not sure how to hold them both.

LUCIA - *Apartment #22, Second Floor*

The building went quiet, just like at the most intense moment at the circus, after the drum rolls. When everyone holds their breath.

Lucia didn't move. Just sat in the grey light, rain streaming down the glass.

Okay, she thought. *No more thinking.*

She lit candles. Opened the windows wider. Let the sound of the rain fill the apartment, the smell of wet pavement, the cool air on her skin.

Then she picked up the saxophone.

Not to answer the question. Not to solve anything. Just to play.

She put her lips to the mouthpiece. Closed her eyes. And let go.

The first notes came low and slow. Searching. The way you reach out in the dark, feeling for the shape of the room.

Then the melody opened. Rose. Spiraled through the apartment like smoke.

She wasn't playing a song. She was playing herself, the weight in her chest, the conflict between head and body, the question before it had words.

Where do I belong?

She played the apartment. The rain on the window. The candles flickering. Daniel's face when he laughed. Her father's voice on the phone, the tremor underneath, *go play your music.* The smoky club on Thursday nights. The kid she taught on Saturdays, who couldn't afford a real teacher but played with more heart than anyone she knew.

She played the life she'd built. Small, yes. Unimpressive, yes. But hers.

The music was pulling toward home. Toward stay. She could feel it gathering, the melody winding down, reaching for the note that would close it. The resolution.

But it didn't come.

Her fingers found a note that didn't belong. Unresolved. Hanging. The kind of note that makes a listener lean forward, waiting for the landing that never arrives.

She knew what that meant. She'd heard it in other players a thousand times. When the music won't resolve, the question remains unanswered.

She held it until her breath ran out.

Then silence. Just the rain.

Lucia lowered the saxophone. Wiped her face. She hadn't realized she was crying.

The music hadn't said stay. It hadn't said go. It had refused to finish the sentence.

She sat with the dissonance. It lived in her chest like a hum.

Someone knocked at the door.

Lucia set the sax down, opened it.

Grace, the woman from next door. Older, gentle, always smiling.

"I made soup," Grace said. "Thought you might want some. Power's out, but it's still warm."

Lucia's throat tightened. She hadn't realized how hungry she was. Or how alone.

"Thank you," she said. "That's... thank you."

Grace handed her the bowl. "You play beautifully, you know. I hear you sometimes. It sounds like the building is breathing."

Lucia blinked. No one had ever said that before.

"I'm glad it doesn't bother you."

"Bother me?" Grace smiled. "Honey, it keeps me company."

After Grace left, Lucia sat on the floor with the soup, crying quietly.

Something in Lucia's chest grabbed onto Grace's words. The building is breathing. A sign. The universe answering what the music wouldn't.

Stay. This is home. The building needs your music.

The dissonance in her chest was quieter now. Grace's words had covered it.

Grace had barely left, and another knock. She thought it was Grace again.

ANJALI - *Apartment #31, Third Floor*

Anjali noticed the sudden silence.

She lit candles. Sat in the middle of the room, cross-legged, watching the light flicker.

She thought about Priya. About the accusation.

And for the first time, she let the question go all the way down.

What if she's right?

Anjali could reach high states. She knew this. Twenty years of practice had given her access to something most people never touched, stillness beneath the chaos, awareness beneath the noise, the place where everything was already whole.

She could sustain it, too. Not just on the cushion. In daily life. Walking through a burning world without crumbling. Being available for others' suffering without collapsing.

But was that presence? Or was it hiding?

She thought about her life. The quiet apartment. The seven students. The father who hadn't spoken to her in twenty years. The phone calls she didn't make. The world outside her window that she watched but rarely entered.

The universe is perfect; she told her students. *Everything is arising and passing.*

But was she holding it? Or avoiding it?

Being present did not mean not showing up. Being present was not a place to hide.

She'd done the shadow work. She knew about bypass. She'd seen it in others, the ones who meditated to avoid their feelings, who talked about oneness while their relationships burned, who reached for transcendence because they couldn't bear to be human.

She'd thought she was different.

But sitting here, in the dark, she wasn't sure anymore.

What if I built a fortress and called it freedom?

What if stillness is just my way of not having to feel how much it all hurts?

What if the universe is perfect AND I'm using that truth to avoid my life?

The rain hammered against the windows. The candles flickered.

She thought about her mother. *You chose a lonely life, Anjali.* She'd always translated that as: *You chose a free life. An awake life.*

But what if her mother saw something she didn't?

What if aloneness wasn't liberation? What if it was the wound she'd never healed?

She sat with it. The worst possibility. Those twenty years of practice had been twenty years of hiding. She remembered the winter she couldn't get out of bed. For weeks. No one came. She'd built it that way.

No answer came.

And then she thought about Grace.

The woman downstairs. The hospice nurse. Dying, and not afraid. Making soup in the middle of a storm. Being here for others even as her own body was failing.

Grace wasn't bypassing. She was IN the mess. Fully, completely, without pretense.

She'd called stillness presence for twenty years. What if she'd been wrong?

She couldn't keep watching.

Something had to change.

SAMIR - *Apartment #32, Third Floor*

Samir barely noticed the power outage. He'd been pacing for hours, the same loop wearing grooves in his mind. Prove it. Can't prove it. Different angle. Still can't. Wrong tool. What tool? Around and around.

He hadn't eaten. Just coffee since before dawn. His body was running on fumes and obsession.

The rain pounded. The room darkened. And still the mind kept spinning, trying to think its way out of a box made of thinking.

You can't explain a non-conceptual experience with concepts.

The thought surfaced and dissolved at increasing speed. Each another wave in the endless churn. It was dizzying.

The dizziness amplified, became physical. The room tilted, the body gave way. For a second, Samir thought it was hunger, but then, no. Way too strong. He grabbed the desk at the last minute, just enough to soften the fall onto the couch. Fear gripped him. What's happening?

In a last moment of clarity, he understood. Repeated "I am safe" before letting go completely.

He saw himself like in a dream. Some unknown place, yet familiar. He was a child, alone. A memory? Not quite. Something lived, but not a memory. The child was playing, yet alone. Playing with itself, changing roles. Creating a fantasy. A dance of characters in his head that would come true in his life.

And then the image dissolved. Black. Emptiness never-ending. The most intense and pure awareness, yet nothing to be aware of. No bliss. A tug. Then an ache. The seed of discomfort slowly growing into intense pressure. Samir knew that pressure. It hovered around without a name, just like a taste, a pinch in the stomach.

And then it came like thunder: Loneliness.

Not human loneliness. Loneliness as an archetype. Something infinitely old.

It was inescapable. It was everywhere, in every atom. In every cell. In every moment. The loneliness expanded and was about to devour everything when a crack happened. A flash. Like a sheet of glass shattering into shards, creating millions of fractals. Life creating itself. Life-creating relationship through self-division under the pressure of loneliness.

The words flashed through him: All One. Alone. The secret hidden in plain sight.

Not the bliss he expected. Something more gutsy. More vital. More real.

Samir opened his eyes. He could suddenly see around him. The flat. The whiteboard. Everything moving, transparent, malleable. He saw the equations dancing around him like cartoon characters. Then the image of the child returned, drawing lines in the sand and waiting for the wave to wash them away. He smiled at the beauty and the futility of it all. No one would tell the child not to draw lines in the sand. His work suddenly looked like those lines. Yet the child expects nothing from drawing. Samir had lost that second part.

He felt nauseous, tense at his core. Just enough awareness to lean forward before he vomited. The same tension he had just experienced, concentrated at his center, now coming out through bile and stomach acid. A strange birth. More like an exorcism. A purge.

Within minutes, he felt better despite the acidic smell and the mess around him. Something had lifted.

The first thought came through, yet thought wasn't the right word. More like a feeling, a sensation with edges that made it palpable. A laughter without sound. Something, almost someone, cracking a joke at his obstinacy.

Like broken pieces falling to the floor before you can catch them.

You. Me. One. Same
Created so I could see.
Alone. All one.
That's what you touched, that aloneness:
that's mine.

That's why any of this exists.

Samir was aware this was his mind speaking or something else wearing his mind's voice. It didn't matter. The words weren't important. The feeling was clear.

He sat for a while on the couch, shaken, trembling. He had crossed a door and come back. Nothing would ever be the same.

The mind was quiet. For the first time in seven years, it had nothing to say.

He didn't need to prove anything.

He knew what mattered now.

MARCUS - *Basement*

Marcus sat in the sudden stillness. His hand played with the flashlight. He didn't need it yet. The darkness was familiar. Eight by ten. Concrete walls. He'd made peace with darkness a long time ago.

He closed his eyes.

The darkness was the same. The cell had been smaller, but the silence was identical. He'd spent three years in that silence. At first, he fought it. Then he broke. Then something else happened.

He touched the bottom beyond despair. A loneliness so total it had no edges. No one to tell. No one to witness. And without a witness, the question came: Do I even exist? If no one sees me, am I real? Days passed where he couldn't be sure. The walls didn't confirm his existence. The silence didn't answer his questions. Just awareness, infinite, with nothing to reflect it back. Nothing to prove it was there.

He understood then why anything existed at all. The loneliness was unbearable. Life was the answer. Every face, every voice, every conflict, God keeping itself company.

He never told anyone. Who would believe him? Who would want to know that underneath everything was an ache that had no cure?

The monitors were company. Every person in the building was a face God made, so it wouldn't be alone. Marcus watched because witnessing was love.

The building was alive around him. He could feel it. Every floor. Every room. Every person.

Ray, in the hallway, sinking. David, in the penthouse, pacing his cage. Yara on the first floor, drowning in what she couldn't save. Grace, sitting with death like an old friend. Lucia, holding her saxophone, afraid to follow where it led. Anjali, still as stone, wondering if stillness had become hiding. Samir, spinning in his head, trying to prove what could only be lived.

All of it moved through him.

The building groaned. Water somewhere, finding its way in. The old bones holding.

He'd sat through worse. The cell. The silence. The night his father died, he played until his fingers bled on chalk.

But this wasn't his storm. It was theirs.

And the building was calling.

Not a sound. A pull. The way you know someone's watching before you turn. The way a mother wakes before the baby cries.

Marcus opened his eyes.

Ray just arrived, "Power's out ' he said. Marcus looked at him without an answer. Truth did not need confirmation. Ray sat on the bottom step.

Time to move.

He picked up the flashlight. Stood slowly.

He walked to the stairs and began to climb.

"Where are you going?" Ray asked.

"Surely someone needs company."

You can't fix life. You can't stop the fire before its time. But you can sit with someone while it burns. You can show up. You can hold the door open. You can be there when they're ready.

The building needed him now.

He climbed.

CHAPTER V - 4:00 PM

By 4 pm, the rain softened. The sky stayed grey, but the violence had passed.

In the building, candles appeared in windows.
Flashlights moved through hallways.

Doors opened that had stayed closed all day.
People began to find each other.
Something was turning.

RAY *- Basement*

The intercom crackled.

Ray was staring at everything falling apart, and there was nothing he could do about it.

"Ray?" Grace's voice, calm and warm. "I went to the market. I made soup. Come up and eat when you have a moment."

He keyed the mic. "I don't have time for..."

"It is ready. Second floor, but you know that."

The intercom clicked off.

Ray stood there, annoyed. He didn't have time for social visits. He had a job to do. The roof was leaking. Yara's sink was still broken. The landlord was going to fire him.

But his stomach growled. He hadn't eaten since yesterday. And with the flooding, no one will be delivering.

Soon after, he climbed the stairs to the second floor.

Grace's door was open. The smell of soup filled the hallway, warm, earthy, real.

She was at the stove, stirring a pot. She looked up when he appeared.

"Come in, Ray. Sit."

He stepped inside, hesitant. The apartment was small, neat. Plants everywhere. Photos on the wall. A candle burning near some family pictures.

She poured soup into a bowl and set it on the table. Gestured to the chair.

He sat. Picked up the spoon.

It was good. Really good. Lentils, carrots, something he couldn't name. He ate without talking.

Grace sat across from him with her own bowl. Didn't say anything.

After a while, Ray said, "I don't know why you're being nice to me."

"Why wouldn't I be?"

"Because I'm..." He stopped. Set down the spoon. "I've been here thirty years. Thirty years of fixing toilets and painting walls and dealing with people who treat me like I'm invisible. And now they're going to fire me. In the middle of a flood. After everything I've done."

Grace nodded.

"It's not fair," Ray said. His voice was tight. "I did everything right. I showed up. I worked. And for what?"

Grace set down her spoon. She took a framed picture near the candle.

"I had a twin sister," she started quietly.

Ray blinked. "What?"

"Her name was Marie. We were born two minutes apart. In the Congo." Grace's voice was steady. "When the war came to our village, we ran. Everyone ran. There was gunfire, explosions, people screaming. We got separated in the chaos."

Ray stared at her.

"I looked for her for three days," Grace said. "Walked through burnt villages, asked everyone I saw. No one had seen her. Eventually, I had to leave. I got on a truck heading to the border. I left without knowing if she was alive or dead."

"Did you… Did you ever find her?"

"No." Grace's eyes were calm. "That was thirty years ago. I still don't know."

Ray felt something twist in his chest. "Thirty years of not knowing?"

"Yes."

"How do you..." He stopped. "How do you live with that?"

Grace was quiet for a moment. Then she said, "Three weeks ago, my doctor told me the cancer came back. Stage four. Six months, maybe less."

Ray's face went white. "What?"

"I'm dying, Ray." She said it simply. Like it was just another fact. "And I'm still here making soup. Because that's what I can do today."

He couldn't speak.

"Loss is loss," Grace said. "You lost thirty years to work you thought would matter. I lost my sister. And now I'm losing my life.

Your pain is real. But it's not special. Everyone has something."

Ray shook his head. "That's not... you're dying, and you're just..."

"Just what? Sitting here? Making soup? Yes." Grace's voice was gentle.

"Because fighting it doesn't change it. And I'd rather spend the time I have left being present than being angry."

"But that's..." Ray's voice cracked. "That's not fair either."

"No. It's not." She paused. "But fair doesn't matter. What matters is what I do with the time I have."

Ray looked down at his bowl. His hands were shaking.

"You think life owes you something," Grace said quietly. "It doesn't. It never did. But that doesn't mean your thirty years were wasted. You showed up. You fixed things. You kept the building standing. That matters, even if no one thanked you."

"But they're going to fire me."

"Maybe. And that will hurt. And you'll grieve it. But you'll still be here. And you'll still have a choice about what you do next." She paused. "I don't have thirty years ahead of me. Maybe you do. And you can spend them bitterly, or you can spend them at peace."

Ray wiped his face with the back of his hand. "I don't know how to do that."

"You don't have to know." Grace's voice was soft. "You just have to stop fighting long enough to see what's actually here."

They sat in silence.

The soup cooled. The rain drummed against the windows.

After a while, Ray said, "I'm sorry. About your sister. About everything."

"Me too." Grace smiled faintly. "But I'm still here. And so are you."

Ray nodded. Stood. Walked to the door.

He paused in the hallway, looked back.

"Thank you," he said. "For the soup."

"You're welcome." Grace's eyes were steady. "You can come back anytime. I always make extra."

Ray nodded again.

And for the first time in thirty years, Ray didn't feel quite so alone.

DAVID - *Hallway, Lucia's Door, Second Floor*

David stood outside Lucia's door for a full minute before knocking.

Second floor. He'd climbed down from the penthouse in the dark, stumbling on the stairs, phone flashlight nearly dead. His shirt was damp with rain. His hands were still shaking.

He could hear her inside. The saxophone, low and mournful, threading through the silence.

He knocked.

The music stopped.

Footsteps. The door opened.

Lucia stood there, her hair pulled back. She looked at him for a moment.

"David?"

"Can I..." His voice cracked. "Can I come in?"

A suitcase sat in the entrance behind Lucia.

He glanced at the suitcase. She stepped aside. "Come in."

The apartment smelled like candle wax. Her saxophone lay on the couch.

She gestured to a chair. He sat. She stayed standing, leaning against the counter.

"How long has it been?" he asked.

"Two years. Almost three."

He nodded. Looked down at his hands. "I didn't know if you would open the door."

"I didn't know you'd ever come."

Silence.

Outside, the rain hammered against the windows.

"I've been up there all day," David said. "Alone. No power, no internet, no…" He stopped. Took a breath. "I was thinking about you."

Lucia didn't answer.

"I think of you often," he said. "Those few weeks… I know it wasn't much. But it meant something to me."

She looked at him steadily. "What do you want me to say?"

"I don't know. Anything. Just…" He stood. "I'm trapped up there. Everything's falling apart. The company, the board, my kids won't talk to me. And suddenly, I thought of you. You're the only person who ever…"

"Whoever what?" Her voice was calm and clear.

"Whoever made me feel like I wasn't..." He stopped. "Like I could breathe for a minute."

Lucia's expression didn't change. "That's not love, David."

"What?"

"Even in those few weeks, you were already calling me fifteen times a day. You showed up at my gigs unannounced. You wanted to know where I was, who I was with, what I was doing every minute." Her voice stayed soft. "That's not love. That's fear."

David heard it. For a second. Then his defense came: "I was afraid of losing you."

"So you tried to control me." She paused.

David felt something collapse in his chest. He sat back down, head in his hands.

"I didn't mean to," he said quietly. "I just... I thought if I could just hold on a little longer, you'd stay."

"You can't hold water like that, David. It just slips through."

They sat in silence.

He looked up.

"I left because staying was killing me." Her eyes were steady. "You wanted me to be yours. But I'm not anyone's. I'm just... mine. And I needed space to remember that."

"And now?" His voice was barely a whisper.

"I wasn't leaving you, David. I was choosing me. And you took that as rejection."

He felt tears rising. "It felt like rejection."

Her voice softened. "But it wasn't. It was just... boundary. I can't be what you need me to be."

David wiped his face. "I don't know how to do that."

"I know."

"Then what do I do?"

Lucia did not answer. David sat in the candlelight, staring at nothing.

After a while, Lucia said, "You can stay here for a while if you want. I have water. Candles. It's quiet."

She looked at him. "I don't need you to be anything other than what you are right now."

David felt something break open in his chest.

He nodded. "Thank you."

Lucia sat down across from him. Picked up her saxophone. "I'm going to play for a bit. Just... be here."

And she played.

Low, slow notes filling the small apartment. Not for him. Not for anyone.

Just the music, moving through her, into the room, into the dark.

David sat and listened.

For the first time in years, he stopped trying to control anything.

He just let it be.

YARA - *Hallway, Anjali's Door, Third Floor*

Yara knocked on Anjali's door.

She was not sure why she'd come up here. The meditation teacher. When the power went out, Yara had felt the walls closing in. She left, like on autopilot.

Anjali opened the door. Calm. Unsurprised.

"Come in," she said. "I just made tea."

The apartment was sparse. Clean. Candles already lit, as if she'd been expecting the darkness. A meditation cushion by the window. Plants. Silence.

Yara sat on the floor, back against the wall. Anjali handed her a cup of tea and sat across from her.

"You're carrying a lot," Anjali said.

Yara laughed, but it came out broken. "Is it that obvious?"

"It's in your shoulders. Your breath."

Yara looked down at her tea. "I tried to help people this morning. Even Ray, the building manager. No one seems to need my help."

My client, Devon, texted me at dawn, saying he couldn't do this anymore. I thought..."
She stopped. Pressed her palms to her eyes. "I spent all morning terrified. And then he texted back that he was fine. He just needed space. Not help. Space."

She took a breath.

"And the world is drowning. Literally drowning. And I'm supposed to just sit here and breathe through it?"

Anjali didn't answer right away.

She just sat. Breathing. Present.

After a long moment, she said, "Why do you need to help?"

Yara looked up. "What?"

"Why do you need to help Ray? Or Devon? Or anyone?"

"Because..." Yara faltered. "Because that's my job. I'm a therapist. People are suffering. I'm supposed to..."

"That's what you do. Not why you need to." Anjali's voice was soft but steady. "What happens if you don't help?"

Yara felt her chest tighten. "Then they suffer alone."

"And?"

"And..." Yara's throat closed. "And I failed."

Anjali waited.

"If I can't help them," Yara said quietly, "then what's the point of me?"

Anjali nodded slowly. "So helping isn't about them. It's about you. About proving you're worth something."

Yara's eyes filled. "That's not..."

"I'm not saying it's wrong," Anjali said gently. "I'm saying it's yours. That need to prove your worth through service, that's your work. Not theirs."

Yara wiped her face. "But people are actually suffering. Ray is actually…"

"Yes. And you can be present with that. But you can't fix it for him. And trying to fix it so you can feel valuable isn't helping him. That's using his pain to avoid your own."

Yara sat in silence, tears streaming.

After a while, Anjali said, "I grew up in Mumbai. Do you know how many people live there?"

Yara shook her head.

"Twenty million. Maybe more. Most of them in poverty that would break your heart." Anjali paused. "When I was young, I thought I had to save them. I volunteered, I worked, I carried their suffering like a sacred duty. And it nearly destroyed me."

"What changed?"

"I realized I couldn't hold twenty million people. I couldn't even hold one person. Not their suffering. Not their healing." Anjali looked at her. "But I could be present without collapsing. And that, just that, was enough."

"But Ray..."

"Ray has food. Shelter. Running water when the pipes work. By Mumbai standards, he's wealthy." Anjali's voice was calm. "And still, he suffers. Because suffering isn't about circumstances, it's about consciousness. And you can't shift someone's consciousness for them."

Yara closed her eyes. "Then what do I do?"

"Your own work." Anjali leaned forward slightly. "You want to help people? Become clear. Do your inner work. Heal your need to prove your worth through saving others. That's the real service."

"That feels selfish."

"It's the opposite. When you're clear, your presence becomes medicine. When you're tangled in your own need to help, you just add more suffering."

They sat in silence.

The candles flickered. Outside, the rain continued.

After a while, Yara said, "I don't know how to do that. My own work."

"Of course you do," Anjali said. "You teach it to your clients every day. Now you just have to apply it." "Your clients are only a mirror for you to look into."

Yara exhaled slowly. She felt something shift in her chest.

"Thank you," she said quietly.

Anjali nodded. "Stay as long as you need."

GRACE - *Apartment #21, Second Floor*

After Ray was gone, Grace washed the bowls. The apartment felt emptier now. The rain had softened. The weight hadn't.

Then a knock. Softer this time.

She opened the door. Samir. The physicist from upstairs. She'd heard him pacing for hours through the ceiling.

"Come in," she said. "I have soup."

Something in her softened. A visitor. Someone to care for. A reason to stop sitting with her own thoughts.

She handed him a bowl. He sat. Ate slowly. Didn't speak.

Grace watched him. There was a stillness in him she hadn't expected. He was not troubled or seeking. He was just present.

They sat in silence. It wasn't uncomfortable. It was the silence of two people who didn't need words to fill the space.

After a while, he looked up.

"Thank you, Grace."

"Just soup."

"Not just soup."

She didn't know what he meant. But she felt it. Something had happened to him. Something she recognized from her years of sitting with the dying. The look of someone who'd crossed a threshold.

"Are you alright?" she asked.

He considered the question. "I am. For the first time in a long time."

She nodded. Didn't push. This, she knew how to do… listening without forcing.

But then he turned the question back.

"What about you, Grace?"

Simple words. But the way he asked… unhurried, undemanding, genuinely curious… something in her chest unlocked.

"I…" She stopped.

He waited. Patient. Still.

"I've been sitting with something all day," she said. The words came slowly. "A photo. My sister. Marie."

"Tell me."

So she did. The promise she'd made... to become a doctor, to go back, to find her. The life she'd built instead. Nursing. Marriage. Children. Her husband's slow death.

"I told myself I was accepting reality," Grace said. "Making peace with what was possible. And maybe I was. But today..." She glanced toward the window. "I watched the news. Children in Congo. My country is bleeding the same way it bled when I left. And I realized I've been carrying my sister for forty-five years, telling myself acceptance was wisdom."

Samir didn't speak. Just listened. The way she had listened to a thousand patients. The way no one had listened to her in a very long time.

"I made peace with dying," she said, quieter now. "But I'm not sure I made peace with how I lived."

"Is there a difference?"

"I think so." She looked at him. "I was ready to die because it meant I could finally stop carrying the promise I didn't keep. Find Marie on the other side. Close the loop without having to fight for it." She paused. "It is surrender, for sure. I'm not sure it's acceptance."

She hadn't said these words to anyone. Hadn't even said them to herself until today.

Samir sat with her in the silence.

"Both can be true," he said finally. "The good life you built. And the life you didn't live."

"Yes." Grace nodded slowly. "Both can be true."

Something released in her chest. Room for both truths to exist without one canceling the other.

"Thank you," she said.

Samir looked surprised. "For what?"

"For asking. No one has asked me that in a very long time."

He finished his soup. Set down the bowl.

"I should go," he said. "But thank you. For the soup. For the silence."

She smiled. "Come back anytime."

He nodded. Walked to the door. Paused.

"Grace?"

"Yes?"

"The life you lived… it mattered. Marie would know that."

Then he was gone.

Grace stood in the quiet apartment. The rain had stopped. The light through the window was softer now.

Both can be true.

She washed his bowl. Put it away. And for the first time all day, the weight in her chest felt lighter.

LUCIA - *Apartment #22, Second Floor*

Another knock. She felt a moment of irritation, after David's visit, she needed space. She opened anyway.

It was Marcus. The night guard. Quiet, always nodding when she passed him in the lobby.

He came in. They talked. Marcus told her his story, Alabama, Dr. King, a church burned, fifty years of music trapped in his head. Then he saw the keyboard in the corner. She watched him sit down, hands trembling. And then he played.

She picked up her saxophone. They played together until something broke open in both of them.

When it ended. Marcus was smiling. She'd never seen him smile before.

Then his eyes moved to the suitcase by the door.

"You going somewhere?"

"I was offered a tour. A chance to join a band. Travel. A different life." She paused. "I won't go. I don't feel it. It does not feel right."

Marcus was quiet. Then:

"I didn't choose to stop playing. Life chose for me." His voice was steady. "You have a door wide open. And you're choosing to close it."

"Maybe not feeling right isn't meaning stay. Maybe you're just scared. Fear and intuition feel the same if you're not careful."

Lucia couldn't speak.

"Don't wake up fifty years from now with music still trapped inside you," Marcus said. "Don't let fear make the choices."

He stood. Walked to the door. Paused.

"The music doesn't need you to stay safe. It needs you to follow it."

Then he was gone. The room felt larger without him. Emptier. But something he'd said was still vibrating in her chest.

Lucia sat in the silence.

The suitcase by the door. The saxophone in her lap.

Everything she'd been sure of an hour ago felt different now.

Marcus had fifty years of silence because he couldn't go. She had a door wide open.

Was she choosing to close it?

She thought of her father. *Go play your music.* That was permission.

She thought of her mother. They didn't cross the desert so she could stay small.

She thought of Grace. The building would keep breathing without her.

Staying had felt true. But maybe it was just fear.

Her hands were trembling. The feeling right before you jump. She picked up her phone. Found Rico's number.

I'm in.

She typed it. Stared at it for a second. Then hit send.

ANJALI - *Apartment #31, Third Floor*

Anjali opened the door to Yara.

The therapist from downstairs. Eyes red, hands shaking.

"I'm sorry to bother you. I just... Can I sit with you for a minute?"

Anjali stepped aside. "Of course."

They sat together on cushions. Anjali didn't ask questions.

But something was different today. She wasn't hovering high above. There was no clarity or certainty. She was next to her. In the dark. Equally lost.

Yara began to talk. About drowning. About clients she couldn't save. About Ray, about Devon, about the world burning while she was supposed to just breathe through it.

Anjali listened. And instead of the clean teaching, she found herself asking a question she didn't know the answer to:

"Why do you need to help?"

The question opened something. Yara's need to prove her worth through service. The desperate belief that she was only valuable if she was giving. The pattern Anjali recognized because she'd lived it herself… twenty-three years old in Mumbai, carrying suffering like a badge of honor until it nearly destroyed her.

She told Yara about Mumbai. About the twenty million. About learning, she couldn't hold even one person's suffering…

The words she'd offered a hundred times. But today, sitting in the candlelight with Yara crying across from her, Anjali heard them differently.

When you're clear.

Was she clear? Or was she hiding behind the pretense of clarity?

Your presence becomes medicine.

Had her presence become medicine? Or had it become a wall she could use to hide?

They sat in silence. The candles flickered. The rain softened.

Yara's breathing slowed. Something had shifted in her... Anjali could feel it.

After a while, Yara stood to leave. Paused at the door.

"Anjali?"

"Yes?"

"How long did it take you? '

"For what?"

"To stop carrying everyone?"

The question rippled in Anjali's chest.

She thought about Priya. About the accusation. About the fortress she might have built and called freedom. About twenty years of practice that might have been twenty years of hiding.

And she told the truth.

"I'm still learning," she said. "Every day."

Yara nodded. Something in her face softened. Like the admission helped more than all the teaching.

She left.

Anjali sat alone in the candlelight.

I'm still learning.

She'd said it to comfort Yara. But hearing the words aloud, she realized they were for herself too.

She did not see failure or confession. Just the truth.

She wasn't done. She didn't have it figured out. Twenty years of practice hadn't made her complete… it had made her more honest about how incomplete she was.

And maybe that was the answer to Priya's question.

What are you actually doing?

Learning. Still. Every day. Showing up without certainty. Showing up without knowing if it was enough. Being present with the not-knowing, instead of above it.

She thought about Grace downstairs. Dying, and still making soup. Still showing up. Not because she had answers. Because she was in it. Fully, completely, until the end.

She thought about Yara… Big-hearted and messy, desperate, drowning Yara… who had just shown Anjali her own reflection without knowing it.

Life wasn't happening to her. It was her. The mess included..

Not just the stillness. The mess too. The doubt. The not-knowing. The student who asks the question that cracks you open.

For Anjali, there weren't many teachers left. Just life. And life had just taught her something through a crying therapist who didn't know she was teaching.

Anjali smiled.

The rain was easing. The candles burned low.

She didn't have it figured out. She never would.

And that, finally, felt like the truth.

SAMIR - *Apartment #32, Third Floor*

The saxophone brought him back.

Slowly. Like surfacing from deep water.

He was on the couch. The room was dark. Rain against the windows. And somewhere below, music. A saxophone, playing something slow and aching.

He sat still. Listening.

His mind was quiet. The endless loop of equations and arguments and counterarguments had stopped. For the first time in years, nothing needed solving.

He became aware of his body. His weight against the cushions. His hands resting on his chest. The rise and fall of breath. Simple things he hadn't noticed before today.

The music moved through him. The musician played like she was praying. He understood that now. Not praying to something… praying as something. The music wasn't separate from her. It was her, pouring out.

That's what he'd been missing.

Not a better argument. Not a more elegant proof. Just this. Being here. In the body. In the moment. Letting life move through instead of trying to capture it with the mind.

He lay there, breathing, listening. Nothing needed to be planned. He just felt alive.

Time passed. He didn't know how long. It didn't matter.

He suddenly noticed something new: he was hungry.

He could stifle his hunger for days. Yet now the body wanted to be fed.

When did he last eat? He could not remember, but today he only had coffee and obsession.

He sat up slowly. The room swayed, then steadied. His legs felt strange beneath him... wobbly, new, like a newborn animal finding its footing.

He remembered Grace. The retired nurse on the second floor. She'd mentioned soup once, weeks ago. "I always make extra."

He didn't want to talk. Didn't want to explain. Just wanted to eat. The aloneness was still in his bones. He needed a face. A voice. Company.

He walked to the door. The hallway was dark, lit only by the dim glow of emergency lights.

He descended the stairs slowly, one hand on the railing. His body still humming with what had happened. Whatever had happened.

He didn't have words for it and did not need any.

He was here.

MARCUS - *Hallway, Lucia's Door, Second Floor*

Marcus had no plan. Maybe it's the music that drew him to knock at Lucia's door first.

His feet just stopped. The saxophone had gone quiet. Something in the silence called him.

He knocked. Lucia opened. She did not look surprised. Like she'd been waiting.

"Just going around," he said. "Making sure everyone's fine."

"I'm okay." She smiled. "I thought you were someone asking me to lower the sound."

"I would never do that." His voice was soft.

"Well, Ray's knocked twice this week," she said with a shrug.

"I know what it feels like to be silenced," Marcus said. "There's nothing more painful than a song left unsung."

Lucia looked at him. "That's... that's beautiful."

He nodded. "It's not mine."

She looked at him curiously. "Do you play?"

"In my head. Only there."

"Why only there?"

"It's no short answer."

"Wanna come in?"

She stepped aside with an inviting arm movement.

Marcus's voice was steady.

Alabama, early sixties. My father was a preacher. He marched with Dr. King."

"I was thirteen when Dr. King was assassinated."

"After that, everything changed," Marcus said. "My father got threats. The church got burned. We had to leave Alabama. Moved to Chicago. My father worked three jobs to keep us fed.

"I'm sorry," Lucia said softly.

"I practiced on a fake keyboard," Marcus said. "Cardboard keys my mother drew for me. I'd sit on the floor and play it for hours. No sound. Just my hands moving. The music was all in my head."

Lucia felt tears rising.

"And it never stopped," Marcus said. "For fifty years, I've been hearing it. Playing it. Just... not with my hands."

Lucia was quiet for a long moment.

His eyes moved to the corner. A keyboard covered by a blanket.

Marcus couldn't stop looking at it.

Lucia followed his gaze. "Wanna try?"

"It's been many years."

He walked to it slowly. Pulled off the blanket. Sat down on the small stool.

His hands hovered over the keys. Trembling.

His mother's hands were drawing cardboard keys on the kitchen table.
The music doesn't need a piano, baby. It just needs you.

His own hands, drawing keys on a board in his cell. Playing silence. Playing grief. How many times had he played for his father's funeral... in his head?

He pressed one key. A single note.

G.

The sound filled the room. Filled his chest. For the first time in fifty years, someone was listening. The aloneness cracked.

His left hand found the bass. His right hand found the melody. And before he knew what he was playing, the hymn was there.

Amazing Grace.

His father's church. Sunday mornings. The congregation swaying. His father's voice, deep and certain, leading them home. He was just a kid.

Marcus played it slow. The way they played it at funerals. The first line. The mourners walking. The weight of loss.

His fingers found the notes they'd played a thousand times in silence. Now, finally freed.

He saw his father's face. The last argument. *Love doesn't stop bullets, Dad.* The door slamming over years of silence. The cell. The guard's voice: *Your father's gone.*

Tears fell on the keys. He kept playing.

I once was lost...

Yes. Lost. For so long.

But now I'm found.

The hymn shifted. His hands moved without deciding. The melody bent, reached, and found another song underneath.

Down by the riverside...

Slower at first. Then building.

Gonna lay down my sword and shield...

The gun he'd held. The fist he'd raised. The war he'd carried for decades.

Down by the riverside...

All of it. Laid down. Finally.

The tempo lifted. The blues crept in. Not sadness anymore, but release. The second line rising, the funeral becoming a parade.

Lucia picked up her saxophone.

Her notes wove through his. Her own saudade meeting his gospel. Tamaulipas meets Alabama. Two griefs, two rivers merging into one ocean.

The music swelled. Filled the apartment. Spilled into the hallway. Drifted through the vents. The building breathing it in.

Marcus' music was a prayer. In its silence, it said:

I'm sorry, Dad. I hear you now. I hear you now.

The second line was full now. Joy and sorrow married. His father's funeral, years late, but finally sung.

Lucia's saxophone soared. Marcus's hands danced. The music carried them somewhere they couldn't go alone.

And then… slowly… it wound down. The tempo easing. The notes spacing out. Breath returning.

One last chord. Sustained. Silence.

Marcus sat with his hands on the keys. Still. Face wet. Chest open.

Fifty years of silence. Finally broken. Finally free.

He looked up at Lucia. She was crying too.

"Thank you," he said quietly. "No one's ever heard it before."

"I heard it before," she said. "Every time you walked past my door."

He smiled. For the first time in a long time, he smiled.

Marcus could hear his father's voice, underneath everything:

There you are, my son.

There you are.

I knew you'd find the way.

Welcome home.

CHAPTER VI - 7:00 PM

By 7 pm, the rain had stopped.

The streets were still flooded, but the water
was receding.
The power stayed out.

Yet inside the building, something had
shifted.
What had broken apart began to settle.

RAY - *Storage room*

Ray sat on the cot.

The basement was no longer filling with
water.
Still a mess. Just not getting worse.

His phone was on the desk. More voicemail.
He still hadn't listened. He should care, but
did not.

Ray pulled off his boots. Wet socks. His feet
ached.

All these years and nothing had changed. Building still falling apart. The landlord still didn't give a shit. World still crushing guys like him.

Same as it ever was.

He lay back. Springs creaked.

Grace's soup had been good. Really good. He couldn't remember the last time someone had fed him. Without asking for anything or complaining. Just soup and a chair.

I always make extra.

Ray rubbed his face with both hands.

She was dying. And she was making soup for the building manager who'd once fixed her sink.

Didn't make sense.

Her sister, lost in the war. Thirty years of not knowing. And she just... lived with it.

Ray thought of his own mother. His sister in Warsaw. He hadn't seen them in decades.

Hadn't called in months. He'd left them behind and told himself it was survival.

Grace had lost someone, too. But she wasn't bitter about it.
Ray didn't understand that. Didn't know how you did that.

But something about it, sitting there, eating soup, her just looking at him like he was a person and not a problem, something about that stuck.

Still getting fired, probably. Still sleeping in a closet. Still invisible.

But someone had said his name today, and fed him.

Tomorrow he'd listen to the voicemails. Deal with whatever shit was coming.

Tomorrow, the building would still be broken, and he'd still be the one they blamed.

But tonight… it was not like he was feeling good, but somehow, less alone. He closed his eyes. His body hurts, but in his chest, that tight thing that had been sitting there for years, there was something different.

Grace said he could come back.

Maybe he would.

DAVID - *Penthouse*

David didn't remember walking back to the penthouse. Somehow, the music had stopped. One moment, he was in Lucia's apartment, the next, he was standing in the dark, hands on the cold glass of his window.

His phone buzzed. He'd forgotten about the phone. The meeting. The board.

He pulled it out. A text: *Meeting happened without you. We'll talk tomorrow.*

David stared at the screen.

His worst fear had happened. And he was still here.

He thought of Lucia. How easily she was moving through her cluttered apartment.

Making life-changing decisions. Navigating opportunities with apparent ease. And she was making music. Lighting candles at peace.

Meanwhile, he'd controlled everything. Optimized everything. Sacrificed everything. His marriage. His kids. His health.

And where had it gotten him?

Alone in a dark building. Missing the meeting that was supposed to save his career.

He thought about Maya's recital. The text he hadn't answered. The college fund that was supposed to mean something.

He thought about his ex-wife. The way she'd looked at him the day she left. Not even angry, just drained. He'd done that. Worn her down until there was nothing left to fight.

He thought about Lucia's words. *You're so afraid of being alone.*

He was afraid of being alone.

And he was alone anyway.

All that control. All that grip.

And he'd ended up exactly where he feared.

Something didn't add up. He was smart. He'd built companies, read markets, and outmaneuvered competitors. But this... this he couldn't solve.

There was something he wasn't seeing.

He didn't know what it was. But for the first time, he knew it was there.

He remembered Lucia handing him a glass of water. "You okay?"

"I don't know," he'd said.

Three words that never came easy.

YARA - *Anjali's Apartment*

Yara stayed.

They didn't talk much. Anjali sat quietly, as if absorbed in something distant. Yara sat with her tea, watching the candles flicker, listening to the rain soften against the windows.

Anjali's words were still turning in her chest.

You're using their pain to avoid your own.

Was that true?

She thought about her client this morning. The one with the manipulative husband. Yara had been there, in her own relationship. Manipulated. She knew how it felt and how much she had wished someone told her the truth at the time. She listened, reflected. But she hadn't told her the truth. Was she avoiding the discomfort?

Why?

Because if she pushed too hard, the client might leave. Might not need her anymore.

And then what would Yara be worth?

She closed her eyes.

All those years in Alexandria. Sensing what people needed. Making guests feel welcome so her mother would smile, so her father would notice, so someone would say *good girl, Yara, you're so helpful.*

She'd built a life on that. A career. An identity.

And underneath it all, the same desperate question: *Am I enough if I'm not giving?*

She didn't have an answer.

Anjali opened her eyes. Looked at her softly.

"How do you feel?"

Yara considered the question. "Lighter," she said. "And scared."

Anjali nodded. "That's honest."

"I am not sure what to do next."

"You don't have to be sure." Anjali stood and moved to the window.

Yara felt her phone in her pocket. She wanted to check if someone had called. If she had a message. She noticed the pull. She held back and did not look.

Tomorrow she would check. Tomorrow she'd see clients again, do the work she was trained to do.

Not to prove anything.

"Thank you," she said again.

Anjali smiled.

Yara stood. Her legs were stiff from sitting so long.

She walked down the stairs in the dark.
Still learning. Everyday

Back in her apartment, the mess was still there. Dishes in the sink. Books unread. The wet towels from this morning still piled in the corner.

But it felt different. Not overwhelming, but more like something simple and clear to do. To start with. One step at a time.

She made tea. Sat by the window. Watched the last of the rain trail down the glass.

Do your own work. Keep learning. Everyday.

For the first time in a long time, that felt like enough.

GRACE - *Apartment #21, Second Floor*

After Samir left, Grace sat in the candlelight.

The rain had stopped. The building was quiet. Something in her was quiet, too.

She thought about what she'd said. Words she'd never spoken aloud. The doctor. MSF. Congo. Marie.

I stopped trying.

For forty-five years, she'd told herself a story: I accepted. I made peace. I found meaning in small things.

And it was true. It was.

But it wasn't the whole truth.

The whole truth was harder. Messier. Two things at once.

She had built a good life. Raised children. Loved a husband. Held the dying with presence and grace.

And she had also let go of something. A dream. A promise. A version of herself that never got to live.

She looked at the photos on the wall. No photos of Marie.

But Marie was here. Had always been here in the space between heartbeats. In the question, Grace stopped asking.

Did I accept? Or did I surrender?

Maybe the answer didn't matter anymore.

What mattered was that she had finally said it. Out loud. To another person.

I wanted more. I didn't do it. And I'm still here.

Grace stood slowly. Her joints ached. The cancer was there.

She wasn't afraid. That hadn't changed.

But something else had.

Before, she was ready to die because it meant the carrying would stop. The promise would dissolve. Marie would be waiting on the other side, and the loop would close.

Now…

Now she saw that it was its own kind of escape.

She didn't want to escape anymore.

She wanted to stay. As long as she had. Present to all of it, the beauty and the grief. The life she'd lived and the life she hadn't.

She walked to the window. The streets were wet. The sky had cleared.

"I'm sorry, Marie," she said quietly. "I didn't come back."

The words hung in the dark room.

"But I'm here now. And I'm not running. I'm right behind you."

She stood there a long time, watching the night.

A patient had told her once, years ago. An old man, days from death, suddenly lucid.

"On your last day, the person you are will meet the person you could have been."

She'd thought about it often. Wondered if it was a warning or just a sadness.

Now she understood.

It wasn't a warning. It wasn't even sad.

It was an invitation. To hold both. To meet that other woman, the doctor, the one who went back, the one who found Marie, and not look away.

Hello. I see you. I'm sorry I couldn't live your life.

But I lived mine.

She turned from the window. Went to the kitchen. Washed Samir's bowl. Put the soup away.

Tomorrow would be another day

She would be here for it. All of it.

LUCIA - *Apartment #22, Second Floor*

The text was sent. Three words. *I'm in.*

Lucia sat on the floor, phone in her lap, staring at nothing.

It was done.

She waited for regret. For panic. For her body to scream *no, take it back.*

Nothing came. Just stillness.

She called her mother.

"Mija? Is everything okay?"

"I'm taking the tour, Mamá."

Silence. Then: "The tour? You said you weren't sure about it?"

"I'm sure now."

Her mother didn't speak for a long moment. Lucia could hear her breathing. Could feel the weight of everything unsaid... the life left behind in Tampico, the desert, the sacrifice, the dreams her mother had buried so Lucia could have this.

"Your father will be proud," her mother said finally. Her voice was thick.

"And you?"

A pause. "I'm always proud of you, mija. Even when I don't understand."

Lucia closed her eyes. "Thank you, Mamá."

"You call us from the road. Every week."

"I will."

After she hung up, Lucia sat with the phone. One more message.

Daniel.

She started typing. Stopped. Started again.

I got offered a tour. I'm taking it. I leave in three weeks. I don't know what that means for us. But I didn't want to disappear without telling you the truth.

Not a kiss instead of an answer. Just honest words.

The apartment was quiet. The candles had burned down to stubs. The rain had stopped.

Lucia looked at the suitcase by the door. Two days ago, she'd packed it. This afternoon, she'd decided to unpack it. Now it was ready to go.

She thought about Marcus. Fifty years of music with nowhere to go. A door that never opened.

She thought about Grace. Dying. At peace. But carrying something unlived.

She thought about David. Gripping so hard he lost everything.

And she thought about herself. The woman who floated, who avoided, who kissed instead of answering.

Not anymore.

The music had asked. And she'd finally said yes.

It would cost her. She knew that. Her father might not be here when she gets back. Daniel might not wait. The life she'd built... small, messy, alive... would change.

But the music didn't need her to stay safe.

She picked up the saxophone. Put it to her lips.

And played.

Not a question this time. Not searching.

Just a sound moving through her, out into the room, into the building, into the night.

The building was breathing.

And so was she.

ANJALI - *Apartment #31, Third Floor*

When Yara left, Anjali didn't return to her cushion.

She stood at the window. Watched the rain ease. The sky lighter now, though still grey.

She thought about writing to Priya. Explaining. Defending. Offering the nuance Priya hadn't seen.

She opened her phone. Started typing.

Dear Priya...

She stopped.

What would she say? That presence wasn't bypassing? That stillness was the ground from which action arose? That you couldn't serve well from a frantic energy?

All true. But not what Priya needed to hear.

Priya needed to burn. To fight. To throw herself against the world's suffering until she learned… the hard way, the only way… that she couldn't carry it alone.

Anjali had walked that path. She couldn't walk it for Priya.

She deleted the message.

Maybe one day Priya would come back. Maybe she wouldn't. Either way, Anjali couldn't chase her. Couldn't convince her. Could only leave the door open.

She set the phone down.

The apartment was quiet. The candles had burned low. The rain had stopped.

What are you actually doing?

The question didn't sting anymore.

Just this: staying in the mess. Breathing. Taking a day at a time. Letting life teach her through whoever walked through the door.

Tomorrow she would sit with her students... whoever came. She would show up. She would teach what she knew. And she would admit what she didn't.

I'm still learning. Every day.

What else could she do?

She looked at her mother's ring. The silver band she'd worn for twenty years.

Don't forget where you came from, beta.

Mumbai. The slums. The girl who wanted to save everyone. The woman who learned she couldn't.

She hadn't forgotten.

She was still that girl.

She was just a person. Uncertain. Here anyway.

Anjali sat down on the floor by the window, where she could see the wet street below and the people starting to emerge now that the rain had stopped.

She breathed.

The world was still burning. She couldn't fix it.

But she was here. Fully here.

And tomorrow, she would begin again.

SAMIR - *Apartment #32, Third Floor*

Samir sat at his desk. Reached for a blank notebook and a pen.

His hand moved.

Something broke today. I have no words for it...

He wrote to Amina first. His Ex-wife. The one who already knew.

Amina,

There is something I want to share. From my heart. Something I have held but never offered.

I see you now. I want to acknowledge you. And apologize.

You remember when you took me to that retreat? I fought it. I thought I knew better. I thought my equations were the path, and your silence was a detour.

You were right. You knew.

You already knew what I just stumbled upon. You held the truth for me, and I was too blind to see it. Too busy looking somewhere else. Too proud to learn from my own wife.

You were a great teacher. I was not humble enough to be a good student.

I'm sorry it took me this long. I'm sorry I chose science over you, over love. I'm sorry I made you feel unseen while I chased something you had already found.

Thank you for not giving up on me… even when you had to leave to save yourself.

I understand now.

Amara,

My daughter. My Angel, my mirror.

You said I waste time on theory while people die. You were right. You have always been right.

I hid in my head because the world was too much. Because feeling was too scary. Because equations don't talk back and don't need anything from me.

But you needed me. And I wasn't there.

I don't have answers. I don't have excuses. I don't have a plan. I just have this: I love you. I'm here now. I want to learn how to be your father.

Sorry it took so long. I'm finally ready.

To Samir

Don't forget this.

The truth doesn't need defending. Only my opinions do.

There's a reason it can't be proven: the search is the point.

The longing is what opens you.

The secret is hidden in plain sight, always there for those who earnestly seek.

Write a book someday. Not a science paper. An invitation for those standing at the edge.

The child draws lines in the sand. The wave washes them away. The child draws again. Stop expecting the lines to last.

The pen stopped.

Samir sat in the silence.

His face was wet. Tears of joy.
Something had emptied out. Something had
filled back in.

He closed the notebook and walked to the
door and down the stairs.

The basement was dark.

Marcus was there.

MARCUS- *Basement Stairs*

Marcus sat on the stairs. Halfway to the
basement.

The building was settling. The fever had
broken. The nervous system was calming.
People in their rooms, sitting with whatever
had shifted.

His hands still trembled. The keys still
dancing in his chest.
His father's funeral. Finally sung.

He felt emptied. Clean like a riverbed after
the flood.

Everyone had walked through something today.

He closed his eyes. His father's presence still there.
Closer than before. He knew he'd never left.

Footsteps on the stairs. Marcus opened his eyes.

Samir came down from above.
They'd sat there before. Many times over the years. Two men in a building full of strangers. Late nights when Samir couldn't sleep. They never talked much.

Something was different this time. The pacing was gone. The spinning. He moved like a man who had stopped running. Marcus recognized the stillness, or rather the rawness that comes right after. He knew that face. He'd worn it himself, walking out of the cell thirty years ago. The aloneness had found another one.

Their eyes met.

Marcus nodded slowly.

"There you are. I see you stopped running."

Samir exhaled. Almost a laugh. Almost tears.

"Yeah. Here I am."

Two men on the stairs. They didn't speak for a long while.

Finally, Samir spoke.

"What now?"

Marcus looked at him. In that look, everything he'd learned. Everything his father had tried to tell him. Everything the cell had taught him. Everything the music had released.

"Now? Just now..."

Samir nodded. Understood.

They sat together. The building holding them.

Marcus felt his father's voice rising in his chest.
Not for him. For whoever needed to hear.

The teaching that took him fifty years to receive.

You can choose. Every moment. Every breath.

Fear or love.

That's the only freedom you'll ever have.

Alors sans avoir rien
Que la force d'aimer
Nous aurons dans nos mains
Amis, le monde entier

"Quand on a que l'amour"
Jacques Brel

PART II The Practice

The Framework as Lived Experience

Thirty years.

That's how long it took me to walk what you just read in a few hours.

The same levels. The same collapses. The same walls I had to hit before I found the door.

The levels aren't just fancy names for a pedantic discourse. They're how we actually grow.

How do we move from blaming everyone to taking charge.

From white-knuckling to letting go.

From feeling alone to seeing yourself in everything.

I don't trust frameworks I haven't bled on. This one has my blood all over it.

Here's how it looked.

How this book creation moved through the levels

For two decades, people told me, "You should write a book."

My inner voice always said, *"Who cares about my story?" It's banal.*

Until I realized it wasn't.

I started writing "seriously" about three to four years ago. Peak moments. Defeat moments. In September 2022, a friend offered to edit my work. She never did, but the offer spurred me into a more dedicated approach. I started at least four major writing projects: a memoir, a movie script, a spiritual book about the stories we tell ourselves, and another during my depression last year.

For all of them, the energy started high and fizzled out.

My Level 1 consciousness kicked in: I collapsed for months, then complained, *I can't write. I don't have what it takes to finish. No one cares anyway.*

These were my Ray moments.

I eventually recovered from the collapse. Changed course. Read all the books about writing, self-motivation, discipline, ass-kicking strategies. I made plans with timelines. I sought productivity hacks. I tied myself to my computer.

The only outcome was backaches and depression.

Those were my David times.

So I dropped the writing. Went back inside to find what was really going on.

I saw that after two very intense years, my nervous system was fried. Stuck in shutdown mode. There was no way to force creativity out of a fried nervous system.

So I designed a self-care plan. Recovery from high stress. Healing from adrenaline addiction.

After just a few weeks of this, one day I sat at my desk and the book flowed out of me like the door of a dam had opened suddenly. I could not stop writing. I had no idea about the structure, the plans, or even what the next chapter would say.

It just came out.

That was my Yara moment, when I saw my fear and was ok with it.

While writing, I suddenly realized that every moment spent over the last four years had been necessary. The material I'd rehearsed many times found its place automatically. I saw that it couldn't be forced. Delays weren't delays; they were maturation.

It was my Grace moment. Literally.

The rest became a completely different story.

The less I worked, the more inspired I was. The best ideas came during hikes, without warning. The more I cared for my nervous system, the less effort it took to write.

That was my Lucia moment, being locked in like a jazz musician during a jam.

It was addictive.

But then another surprise came.

Although I'd studied this material for years and thought I knew it all, I realized the book was a mirror. It showed me things I did not want to look at. All the lingering aspects of early-stage development I was still carrying: self-judgment, fear of failure, doubt that I had what it takes.

The book had pulled the carpet from under my feet.

It was my Anjali moment.

The book came out so quickly, so effortlessly, that suddenly something became apparent: there was no limit to what I could write. Neither in content nor in quantity.

From that place, everything was possible. It wasn't me creating. Call it God, call it flow, call it whatever, I was just the typist.

That was my Samir moment.

Maybe I haven't met my Marcus moment yet, since I'm determined to publish this book. But I know that looking back is always easier than looking into a future that doesn't exist yet.

The story I held for decades is now out of me. And it may sound weird, but it felt like I had left the trash by the curb, and my house was cleaner for it.

Carrying an untold story is exhausting.

And while this one is now written, I know I have much more to write. I won't hold myself back anymore.

I started *Locked In* my own stories.

I ended *Locked In* a creative groove.

The only thing that changed was my reading of what was already there.

How my life moved through the levels

In my early years as a teenager and young adult, I was struggling with the world I'd been dropped into. Stubborn. Rebellious. I'd been betrayed too many times, bullied, violated, and misled. So I was angry. Defensive. Always on guard.

In that dynamic, I couldn't see yet that I was caught in what I now call the victim triangle: perpetrator, savior, or victim. Whatever role I took, I was ultimately always in victim consciousness.

That was stage 1 (Ray).

As I grew tired of that situation, I started exerting control over my environment. Wherever and whenever I could take control, I would. I became a guide because that's a good place to direct others. I'd learned to function in dysfunction, and I was determined to make it my best skill. Unconsciously, of course.

That was stage 2 (David).

I stayed in this space for many years. The world paid me well for it.

One day, I woke up, and it felt totally off. Somehow, I'd betrayed what I stood for in the process. So I resigned from the whole career thing and picked up a pilgrim's stick. I did many things, meditation, fasting, silence, but mostly I took responsibility for what had happened in my life.

And that alone changed everything.

That was stage 3 (Yara).

But the path didn't protect me from life. On the contrary.

With my new legs, I made many mistakes. (I don't see them as mistakes anymore, but that's for later.) Lost a lot of money. Damaged relationships. Until there wasn't much left to protect.

I was at the bottom of the hole. Dark years.

But every time I crashed, I saw a rebound. A pattern. Contraction and expansion.

That was stage 4 (Grace).

So I grew. And as I did, more and more people came asking me how I'd done it.

I started sitting with others, observing their lives as they are now. I did it so many times that the faces vanished, but our shared story remained visible.

I was back to being a guide, but this time not out of control. Out of peership. For all my fellow humans.

That was stage 5 (Lucia).

In the process, I realized that my inner states were what generated the most transformative momentum for others. Self-care became the best thing I could do for the world.

Suddenly, there was no "other" anymore. I could see clearly: my inner states influenced the outer elements.

That was stage 6 (Anjali).

This spurred me to work in a different way. Writing is one of them.

That was stage 7 (Samir).

Here I am. I don't know where the road goes from here.

Don't tell me. I don't want to hear it.

After all, didn't we sign up for an adventure? And if I knew the path, wouldn't it be boring?

So when a meditation app sends me notifications, you know the stuff, "I am the journey, the path, the walker, the arrival, not separate" with flying unicorns farting rainbows, that is where I turn off the damn thing.

When we have no clue what just happened.

That is stage 8 (Marcus).

Seeing the Levels Everywhere

When I think of **Level 1**, what comes to mind is George Orwell's 1984 or the stories of Anne Frank and Elie Wiesel. How could anyone not feel purely in a victim position when caught in a carceral system or concentration camp? That is probably the feeling of every child on a battlefield anywhere in the world today. And where else to start but first to be acknowledged for our misery, and at least hope that our sacrifice is not in vain?

When I think of **Level 2**, *Heart of Darkness* by Joseph Conrad comes to mind, and it may surprise you, but also Steve Jobs and

Margaret Thatcher. They built empires, yes, but at enormous cost to everyone around them. Incredibly powerful, but blind to the price of their dominance through their insatiable appetite for power and inability to surrender.

When I think of **Level 3**, I think of Ishmael, the gorilla in Daniel Quinn's book, teaching a human that the story we tell ourselves about civilization shapes the reality we live in. 'There is no one right way to live,' he says. We are not separate from nature. We just believe we are. And that belief creates everything that follows. Brené Brown and Michael Singer built careers on this same insight: change your inner state, change your life. Because the story we tell ourselves becomes the world we inhabit.

Level 4 brings *The Alchemist* by Paulo Coelho and Viktor Frankl as the hero of his own journey in *Man's Search for Meaning*, finding meaning at any cost, even in the darkest places on earth. This is where we learn that difficulty isn't punishment. It's teaching.

Level 5, calls *The Prophet* by Kahlil Gibran, of course. One of my favorite books ever. And Maya Angelou, who became a vessel for something much larger than herself, letting wisdom flow through. At this level, we stop forcing and start listening.

Level 6 calls to mind my favorite poet, Rainer Maria Rilke, writing letters to himself about his own inner journey. And Carl Jung and Eckhart Tolle, both devoted to making the unconscious conscious. Here, we recognize: the world is our mirror. Change within, and the outer shifts. Not metaphorically. Literally.

Level 7 honors my compatriot Antoine de Saint-Exupéry and *Le Petit Prince*, a book that filled my childhood with the possibility of wisdom-filled sheep even in the depths of the desert, facing your own demise. And humans like Nikola Tesla, Buckminster Fuller, and Terence McKenna, whose imaginative genius nothing could stop. Consciousness as infinite possibility. Reality as malleable. The future unwritten.

Level 8 gets more difficult. For me, only the *Tao Te Ching* works at this level. "When nothing is done, nothing remains undone." How can we get beyond this? And humans like Ramana Maharshi or Thich Nhat Hanh, to choose a more contemporary person. At this level, there is no separation. Just presence.

Yet these are only snapshots. Pictures to point in a direction and help us navigate. Human nature and psyche are far too complex to be reduced to these little stamps.

Take, for example, my lifelong heroes: Martin Luther King Jr., Nelson Mandela, Mahatma Gandhi, and the Dalai Lama. In the course of their lives, they traveled through the layers, starting with control and force in their early years, only to reach the greatest heights after patiently journeying through all the levels.

That's the real teaching. Not that you should "be at Level 8." But that evolution is possible. That the levels aren't labels, they're doorways.

The question isn't which level you've reached.

It's whether you're willing to keep playing.

207

PART III The Framework

The 8 levels

The Victim (Level 1: Life Happens TO Me)

At this level, consciousness experiences itself as powerless. The world feels random, cruel, controlled by forces beyond influence. The dominant emotions are hopelessness, resentment, and fear. The belief is simple and total: *I am a victim of circumstances I didn't choose and can't change.*

This level often emerges from real powerlessness, childhood trauma, systemic oppression, and repeated failure despite effort. The pain is legitimate. The anger is justified. But the consciousness gets stuck in a loop: *because nothing I do matters, I stop trying. And because I stop trying, nothing changes, which proves nothing I do matters.*

The shadow of this level is the refusal of responsibility, not out of laziness, but out of self-protection. If I claim agency and fail again, the wound deepens. Safer to stay in blame.

The gift, however, is that when this pain is seen without being fixed, it can become fuel. What's needed isn't advice or fixing, it's presence.

You saw this when Ray sat in the flooded basement, head in his hands, saying: "Thirty years. And it all came down to this." Ray couldn't see his own agency. The building was falling apart, yes. But his belief that *nothing he did mattered* kept him paralyzed. Grace didn't argue with him. She didn't try to convince him he was wrong. She just sat with him, told him about her own losses, and said: *"Your thirty years mattered, even if no one thanked you."* That witnessing, not fixing, was enough. Something moved.

The transition out of Level 1 begins when someone sees you without trying to change you. When the pain is acknowledged, not dismissed, that's when agency, quiet, tentative, can begin to emerge.

The Controller (Level 2: Life Happens BY Me)

At this level, consciousness discovers agency and immediately weaponizes it. The belief is: *If I control enough, I'll be safe. If I work hard enough, force things into place, and manage every variable, I can prevent chaos.* The dominant emotions are anxiety masked as productivity and fear disguised as ambition.

This level often emerges as a necessary correction to Level 1's helplessness. The person realizes: *I'm not powerless. I can DO something.* And so they do, relentlessly. But the doing comes from fear, not trust. The relationship to reality is one of domination: life must be managed, optimized, controlled.

The shadow of Level 2 is exhaustion. Burnout. The inability to relax. Surrender feels like weakness. Connection feels like vulnerability. The controller creates the very chaos they're trying to prevent, through force, through micromanagement, through the refusal to let anything simply be.

The gift of this level is genuine: it gets things done. It builds systems. It takes initiative. The world needs this energy, but only when it's balanced with trust rather than driven by terror.

You saw this when David stood in his penthouse, powerless, trying frantically to connect to the board meeting that would decide his fate. He'd spent his entire life controlling his company, his relationships, even Lucia, whom he'd loved but couldn't hold without gripping. When the power went out, and he was trapped, all his strategies failed. He had no move to make. For the first time in years, he had to just... be. And it terrified him. Later, when Lucia told him, *"You wanted to own me, not love me. Love is spaciousness, not grip,"* she named the core wound of Level 2: the belief that safety comes from control, when experience shows, it comes from letting go.

The transition out of Level 2 begins when control fails so completely that there's no choice but to surrender, when the exhaustion becomes unbearable. When someone, like Lucia, shows you that grip isn't love.

The Creator (Level 3: Life Happens IN Me)

At this level, consciousness turns inward. The realization is destabilizing: *I create my experience through my beliefs, my choices, my inner state.* The world is no longer something that happens TO me (Level 1) or something I must dominate BY force (Level 2). It's something I shape from within.

This is the pivot point. The moment consciousness wakes up to its own agency, not as force, but as responsibility. The dominant emotion is empowerment mixed with accountability. Sometimes it tips into self-blame: *If I create my reality, then my suffering is my fault.* But at its best, Level 3 is about radical honesty: *I can't control what happens, but I can control how I respond. And that response shapes everything.*

The shadow of Level 3 is self-absorption. The tendency to make everything about inner work. Sometimes this level blames itself for systemic issues; *if I just thought differently, this wouldn't be happening.* It can slip into bypassing: *just change your thoughts, and everything will be fine.* This ignores the reality of external systems, power structures, and forces beyond individual control.

The gift of Level 3 is immense: it takes radical responsibility. It does the inner work. It breaks victim patterns. It recognizes that suffering often comes not from circumstances, but from the stories we tell about circumstances.

You saw this when Yara sat in Anjali's apartment, overwhelmed by her need to fix everyone, Ray, Devon, and the world. She'd absorbed their pain, made it hers, and was drowning under the weight of it. When Anjali asked, *"Why do you need to help?"* Yara realized: her helping wasn't about them. It was about proving her own worth. *"If I can't help them, then what's the point of me?"* That's Level 3's work, recognizing that the external crisis (Ray's collapse, the client's despair) is triggering an internal wound (her need to be needed). Anjali didn't tell her to stop caring. She told her to stop carrying: *"You can be present with someone without making their pain yours. The work isn't fixing them. It's healing your need to fix them."*

The transition out of Level 3 begins when you realize that doing all the inner work, taking all the responsibility, still doesn't give you control. Life remains unpredictable. Painful things still happen. And at a certain point, the question shifts from *"What did I do wrong?"* to *"What is this trying to teach me?"*

The Receiver (Level 4: Life Happens FOR Me)

At this level, consciousness makes a radical reframe: *Everything serves my evolution. Chaos has hidden order. Difficulty contains wisdom.* The belief is no longer that life is against you (Level 1), or that you must force it into submission (Level 2), or even that you create it through your thoughts (Level 3). Instead, life is intelligent. It's guiding you, even through pain.

This is not bypassing. It's not pretending that suffering doesn't hurt or that injustice is fine. It's a deeper trust: that even the hardest experiences can crack you open in ways that lead to growth. The dominant emotions are gratitude, acceptance, and trust, not because everything is easy, but because we've learned to see the pattern beneath the chaos.

The shadow of Level 4 is that it can become passive. It can slip into platitudes: *everything happens for a reason* as a way to avoid legitimate anger or necessary action. It can bypass real suffering by wrapping it in language that doesn't actually honor the wound.

The gift of this level is trust. It sees meaning in difficulty. It reframes obstacles as teachers. It can hold complexity without collapsing into fear or control. It doesn't need life to be fair; it just needs to stay present to what is.

You saw this when Grace sat with Ray and told him about losing her twin sister in the war, thirty years of not knowing if Marie was alive or dead, and then, quietly, that she was

dying of cancer. Six months, maybe less. Ray couldn't comprehend it. How could someone facing death, someone who'd lost everything, still be making soup? Still sitting with him? Still at peace? Grace didn't minimize the pain. She didn't say it was all fine. She said: *"Loss is loss. You lost thirty years to work you thought would matter. I lost my sister. And now I'm losing my life. Your pain is real. But it's not special. Everyone has something."* She wasn't dismissing his suffering; she was showing him that suffering doesn't have to destroy you. That you can grieve and still show up. That life doesn't owe you fairness, but it also isn't punishing you. It just is.

The transition out of Level 4 begins when trust deepens beyond acceptance. When you stop just *receiving* what life gives you and start sensing that you're a co-creator, not through force, but through listening.

The Channel (Level 5: Life Happens THROUGH Me)

At this level, consciousness becomes a vessel. The belief shifts: *I am not the author of my life, I am the channel. Something larger moves through me. Alignment matters more than ambition. Surrender is the path.*

This is where effort becomes flow. Where doing comes from being. The person at Level 5 doesn't force outcomes. They listen, sense, attune, and then act, not from the ego's agenda, but from what is asking to happen. The dominant emotions are surrender, flow, and spontaneity. There's movement, but it's not frantic. There's direction, but it's not rigid.

The shadow of Level 5 is that it can struggle with practical reality. Money, structure, boundaries, these can feel heavy, mundane, inconvenient. There's a risk of floating rather than grounding. Of waiting for perfection instead of taking messy, imperfect action. Of avoiding necessary confrontation because it doesn't "feel" right.

The gift of this level is grace. Effortless creation. Moving with life instead of against it. Trusting intuition. Acting from feel, from gut, not pressure. When someone at Level 5 creates, it feels like the work is doing itself.

You saw this when Lucia woke to the sound of rain and had to decide: take the tour or stay. The tour was everything she'd worked for, three months across the country, then Europe, playing with one of the best musicians in the world. But it didn't feel aligned. She didn't analyze it. She didn't make a pros-and-cons list. She picked up her saxophone and played. For hours, the question moved through her. Not as thought. As music. Later, after sitting with Marcus, after watching Grace hold death without flinching, after seeing David's grip shatter, something shifted. She texted Rico: "I'm in." Called her mother: "I'm taking the tour." Her father might not be there when she got back. Daniel might not wait. But the music didn't need her to stay safe. It needed her to follow. When she played that final time, it wasn't a question anymore. It was a *yes.*

The transition out of Level 5 begins when surrender deepens into recognition. When you stop experiencing yourself as separate from what's moving through you. When you stop knowing where you end, and it begins.

The Mirror (Level 6: Life IS Me)

At this level, the separation collapses. Consciousness realizes: *There is no "out there" that isn't also "in here." The world is my mirror. Inner and outer are one. Being precedes doing.*

This is nondual awareness. Not a philosophy in the head, but as lived experience in the body. The person at Level 6 doesn't just believe consciousness creates reality; they *see* it, mechanically, moment by moment. When their inner state shifts, the outer world reflects it. Not magically. Not metaphorically. Literally.

The dominant emotion is clarity. Presence. An unshakeable knowing that what you are *being* is what you are creating. There's no more seeking. No more trying to become. Just presence. And from that presence, right action arises, not from effort, but from seeing what is.

The shadow of Level 6 is its tendency to become self-absorbed. It can underestimate systemic forces. It can slip into *"just meditate, and it'll all work out"* without engaged action. It can forget that not everyone is operating from this level of awareness, and that meeting people where they are is part of the work.

The gift of this level is radical responsibility. Not for fixing the world, but for being coherent. For clearing distortions. For recognizing that the state of the world is, in part, the state of our consciousness. And the state of our consciousness is something we can shift, right now.

You saw this when Anjali sat with Yara and didn't try to fix her overwhelm; she just reflected it back. *"You're trying to carry it all. You can't.*" Yara wanted tools, strategies, answers. But Anjali gave her something simpler and harder: presence. She didn't absorb Yara's pain. She didn't take it on. She just sat there, clear, grounded, unshakeable, and let Yara see her own pattern. When Yara asked, *"How do you just sit with all of this and not collapse?"* Anjali said, *"I don't try to fix it. I don't try to carry it. I just let it move through. And I trust that being present is enough."* That's Level 6. Not transcendence. Not bypassing. Just clarity. Being steady enough that others can lean against you.

The transition out of Level 6 begins when presence expands beyond the personal. When you recognize that consciousness isn't just ours, it's the field itself. And we can participate in shaping reality not through individual will, but through resonance with infinite possibility.

The Architect (Level 7: I Am INFINITE)

At this level, consciousness recognizes itself as boundless. Reality is no longer fixed; it's fluid, participatory, quantum. The belief is:

Consciousness is primary. Matter is secondary. What I perceive, what I imagine, what I hold in awareness, these shape what collapses into form.

This is where science meets mysticism. Where the observer effect scales beyond the laboratory. The person at Level 7 understands that the future isn't predetermined. Every moment is a field of infinite potential. What manifests depends on where awareness is placed, what beliefs are held, and what imagination dares to conceive.

The dominant emotion is wonder. Awe. Creative power. A sense that anything, truly anything, is possible. The limitations we experience are not the limits of reality. They're the limits of what we've been willing to imagine.

The shadow of Level 7 is that it can lose grounding. It can become so absorbed in possibility that it forgets embodiment. It can drift into abstraction, theory, and conceptual understanding without lived practice. It can struggle with ordinary life, bills, relationships, the mundane, because the mind is always in the stars.

The gift of this level is vision. The ability to perceive solutions beyond linear thinking. To see through limitations. To hold possibilities that haven't yet manifested. To recognize that consciousness doesn't just observe reality, it participates in creating it.

You saw this when Samir spent the entire day spiraling about whether to publish his paper, seven years of work pointing toward one conclusion: consciousness participates in creating reality. He had the framework. He had the math. But he couldn't prove it the way physics demanded. His mentor told him, "Maybe physics isn't the right tool. Maybe pointing is enough." His daughter had already told him the harder truth: "You waste time on theory while people die." He paced for hours, the mind trying to think its way out of a box made of thinking. Then the veil lifted. Not slowly. Like a detonation. The boundaries dissolved. He wasn't in the room anymore. He WAS the room. The rain. The equations. His daughter's anger. All of it, one event. When he came back, face wet with tears, he understood: the inquiry itself was the point. Not legacy. Not validation. Just the love of the mystery. Samir had spent his life in abstraction, theories, equations, and models of consciousness. But he'd forgotten to live it. Later, he wrote the letters he'd never written: to his ex-wife, apologizing for not learning from her; to his daughter, apologizing for hiding in his head while the world needed him present. When he sat with Marcus in the basement, Marcus said simply: "You stopped running." That's the work of Level 7: translating infinite possibility into presence. Bringing the sky down to ground.

The transition out of Level 7 begins when we recognize that we are not separate from the infinite field we've been studying. That consciousness isn't something we *have*, it's what we *are*. And that's not a concept. It's an experience we can't unfeel.

The One (Level 8: I Am ENERGY)

At this level, there is no separation. Consciousness recognizes: I am not in the universe. I am the universe. There is no observer and observed. Just one field.

At this level, there's nothing to say that doesn't sound like a bumper sticker or an Instagram meme that you've read a thousand times. It is like all these quotes the Buddha is supposed to have said, while he is not around to deny, nor did he ever write a single line himself.

So I won't try. We either recognize it or we don't.

Words point. They don't arrive.

The shadow of Level 8 is that it can look like detachment. Dissociation. It may not function well in ordinary life. There's a risk of abandoning the human dimension entirely, forgetting that embodiment still matters, that people still suffer, that showing up in form is part of the work. Unity without compassion becomes coldness.

The gift is liberation. No suffering from separation. No fear of death, death is just a form changing shape. The self recognizes it was never separate to begin with.

You saw this when Marcus sat in the dark basement as the power went out, flashlight on the desk, untouched. He didn't panic. He didn't react. He just sat. The building was flooding. People were scared. Ray was collapsing. But Marcus held it all, not by doing, but by being. When he climbed the stairs, it wasn't because someone called. It was because he felt the building calling to him. When Ray asked, "Where are you going?" Marcus said simply: "Someone needs help." He didn't know who. He just knew. Later, when Lucia heard his story, fifty years of unplayed music, and they sat at the keyboard together, blues pouring out of him like water held back for decades, Marcus wasn't playing for anyone. He was just letting the music move. The music was him. The building was him. The grief, the release, the breath, all one thing.

There is no transition out of Level 8. Not because there's nothing beyond, but because seeking stops. What's left isn't something you can describe. Only live.

Where is This Going?

Imagine a world where Ray, broken, bitter, invisible, walks into a community center and someone asks him not "what do you do?" but "what are you learning about yourself right now?" Where his thirty years of showing up, of fixing what kept breaking, of carrying what no one else saw, where all of that is witnessed. And in that seeing, Ray realizes: I'm not a victim of my circumstances. I'm the one who chose to stay. And that choice mattered.

Imagine a world where David's board meeting doesn't start with revenue projections, but with a moment of silence. Where the opening question isn't "how do we dominate the market?" but "what are we actually trying to create here?" Where his compulsion to control, the thing that built his company and destroyed his marriage, is recognized not as strength, but as unintegrated fear. And instead of shaming him for it, someone just asks: "What would it feel like to let go? Just for five minutes. What would happen if you trusted?"

Imagine Yara opening her therapy practice and the first thing clients see isn't a list of credentials, but a simple sign: "This is your work, not mine. I'm just the witness." Where boundaries aren't seen as coldness, but as the most compassionate thing you can offer. Where her need to fix, to save, to prove her worth through healing others, where all of that is gently reflected back to her by a community that says: You're allowed to exist without justifying it.

Imagine Grace's cancer diagnosis not met with pity or the frantic scramble to fight and beat it, but with presence. Where her doctor sits with her and says, How do you want to spend the time you have left? Where hospice isn't a failure of medicine, but a recognition that death is part of life. Where her thirty years of sitting with dying people, of learning that resistance creates more suffering than death itself, where all of that is honored, not as defeat, but as mastery.

Imagine Lucia playing her saxophone on a street corner and someone stopping, not to drop a dollar, but to sit down and listen for twenty minutes. Where music isn't background noise or entertainment product, but recognized as what it actually is: a language for the unspeakable. Where her decision to go or stay isn't about duties or ambition, but about following what she feels, where her parents, who crossed a desert so she could have stability, finally understand: she found a different kind of safety. The kind that comes from being true.

Imagine Anjali teaching meditation, and no one asks, "What will this get me?" Will it make me more productive? Less anxious? Better at my job? Imagine instead they ask: Will this help me see what's actually true? Where her years of practice, of getting out of her own way, where all of that isn't dismissed as navel-gazing or privilege, but recognized as the work. The work that doesn't fix the outer world directly, but shifts the place where action actually comes from.

Imagine Samir publishing his paper, or not publishing it, and either way, it's fine. Where his seven years of proving that consciousness creates reality aren't judged by citations or tenure or legacy, but by whether he lived it. Where the question isn't: did you contribute to human knowledge? But did you become more conscious? Where the mind finally stops trying to "think its way out". Where he writes the letters he never wrote: to his ex-wife, thanking her for knowing what he was too proud to learn; to his daughter, apologizing for hiding in abstraction while she needed him present. Where his mentor's words finally land: "Maybe proof isn't the point. Maybe seeking is enough."

Imagine Marcus sitting in the basement, holding the building the way he's always held it, and everyone in that building knowing, not intellectually, but in their bones, that his part is important. That his presence, his stillness, his fifty years of unplayed music, finally released, that all of it matters. Not because it produces anything. Not because it achieves anything. But because it is. Because he is. And being is enough.

PART IV The Stakes

This isn't utopia. Suffering won't disappear. Conflict won't end.

But we could live in a world that understands Level 2 isn't the top. That control, force, domination, endless growth, these aren't the pinnacle of human evolution. They're a stage. Necessary. But not final.

The shift doesn't require everyone. It never has. Slavery ended. Women got to vote. Civil rights moved. Marriage equality happened. Not through universal agreement, through critical mass. Enough people saying: This doesn't work anymore. We're choosing differently.

We're at that edge now. The old systems are cracking. Climate. Economy. Politics. The question is: collapse or transformation?

Why Levels of Consciousness Matter

The future isn't something that happens TO us. That's Level 1. The future isn't something we force into being. That's Level 2. The future is something we become, and then watch it show up around us.

If we want a different world, we must become a different consciousness.

In the 1950s, US psychologist Clare Graves began a thirty-year study to understand why people think and act so differently. His research, later developed into Spiral Dynamics, mapped eight levels of human consciousness, from survival instinct to universal awareness.

The framework in this book is adapted from Justin Faerman's *Mapping the Evolution of Consciousness: A Holistic Framework for Psychospiritual Development*—a synthesis of Maslow, Graves, Wilber, Hawkins, and others' work alongside many original insights and findings from his own research and practice into a coherent map of human development. His work gave me the structure. The characters gave it life. For those who want to go deeper into the research, visit https://www.justinfaerman.com/research/

The numbers are sobering.

According to Graves' research, roughly 90% of the world's population operates from what he called Red, Blue, and Orange consciousness: power, rules, and achievement. In the framework used in this book, that's all, Level 2. Control. Dominance. Life happens BY me.

These levels hold 85% of the world's power.

Meanwhile, consciousness beyond control, Levels 3 through 8 in the framework used in this book, accounts for 10% of the population. The remaining 15% of power.

This isn't just interesting. It's the answer to a question most people haven't thought to ask: Why do our problems persist?

Climate collapse. Economic inequality. Political polarization. These are Level 2 problems. They were created by control-based consciousness: extract, dominate, win. And we keep trying to solve them with the same consciousness that created them. More control. Better strategy. Smarter domination.

It doesn't work. It can't work. You can't solve a problem from the level that created it.

I hold a post-graduate degree in Political Science from La Sorbonne and spent three decades in international development. Here's what you probably never heard: democracy in its current form doesn't help.

Democracy elects leaders who reflect the majority. If 90% of voters operate from Level 2, they elect Level 2 leaders. Leaders who promise control, certainty, and dominance. Leaders who see the world as something to be managed, not understood.

I've watched this pattern for decades. And I'm tired of it. We've been stuck here for 10,000 years.

Before agriculture, humans lived in small bands. Then we learned to grow food, claim land, and build walls. Control became possible. Control became necessary. And control became the operating system for civilization.

Every empire since has run on the same code: dominate or be dominated. The technology changed. The consciousness didn't.

Graves' research is fifty years old now. The percentages may have shifted. But the pattern holds. Look around. The world is still run by people who believe the answer to every problem is more control. The Davids of our story.

The question is not so much whether this is true. The question is what we do about it.

Working With The Framework

So how do you actually use this?

Recognize where you live. Not where you visit in meditation or peak experiences, but where you go under stress. When a relationship ends, where do you land? When a project fails, what's your default? When the world feels chaotic, how do you respond?

That's your baseline.

There's no shame on any level. Level 1 isn't bad; it's often a rational response to real powerlessness. Level 2 isn't failure, it's necessary agency. Every level has gifts and shadows. The work isn't to skip levels. It's to complete them.

If you're at Level 1, find one place where you have agency. One choice that's yours. That's the bridge to Level 2.

If you're at Level 2, notice what you're trying to control. Ask what's beneath it. Usually fear. And beneath fear, something that needs to be seen, not fixed. That's the bridge to Level 3.

If you're at Level 3, drowning in self-improvement, ask: What am I trying to prove? The bridge to Level 4 is realizing you don't have to earn your right to exist.

Each level has its work. You cross it not by force, but by completion.

Use the quiz. 48 questions to reveal your baseline, your stress patterns, your expansion potential. It's not about labeling yourself. It's about seeing yourself. You can't evolve from a place you can't see.

Find the Quiz link on the next page.

Take it. Sit with it. Notice what surprises you, what you resist. Then use it as a map: "Oh, I regress to Level 1 under financial stress. Good to know. That's where the work is."

Find support. This isn't meant to be done alone. Ray needed Grace. David needed Lucia. Yara needed Anjali. We don't grow in isolation. We grow in encounters.

The Invitation

Start where you are.

Not where you wish you were. Not where you think you should be. Where you actually are.

Stay there until it's done with you. Don't rush. Don't bypass. Don't leapfrog to Level 8 because it sounds more evolved. The levels aren't a ladder out of your humanity. They're how you walk deeper into it.

Do the work.

Whatever that looks like. Therapy. Meditation. A long walk where you finally think the thought you've been avoiding. Sitting with a friend and saying: I don't know who I am anymore, and I'm scared. Quitting the job that's killing you. Starting the project you've been avoiding. Forgiving the person you swore you never would.

Not because it'll save the world.

But because it'll save you.

And a you that's faced your own bullshit, a you that knows your patterns and isn't run by them anymore, that you can actually be useful.

––––––––––––––––

The book is ending. Your work is beginning.

The characters are fictional. Your life is real.

The crisis in the story is a metaphor. The crisis in the world is here.

And the question, the only one that matters, is this:

The trap, or the groove?

The lock, or the key?

You already know.

This book showed you eight people experiencing the same day from eight different levels of consciousness.

Now it's your turn.

This quiz won't tell you who you are. It will show you where you stand - under pressure, in relationships, in the quiet moments when no one's watching.

48 questions. Brutal honesty required. Take it when you're ready to see.

https://www.lockedinthebook.com/quiz

ABOUT THE AUTHOR

Gabriel Lovemore holds a post-graduate degree in Political Science from La Sorbonne, specializing in International Development. He spent three decades working with NGOs and the UN across 70 countries: Europe, Africa, Asia, and the Americas. In 2007, he left that world to teach yoga in India. Ten years later, he moved to Los Angeles, where he now works as a consciousness coach.

He's still in it. Still learning.